About the author

Linda Newbery taught English in various schools before becoming a full-time author, and a regular tutor of writing courses for children and adults.

She has written a number of books for young adults, and has been twice nominated for the Carnegie Medal, and also the Writers Guild Award.

Linda lives in Northamptonshire with her husband and three cats.

The *Moving On* trilogy by Linda Newbery

No Way Back
Break Time
Windfall

ORCHARD BOOKS
96 Leonard Street, London EC2A 4XD
Orchard Books Australia
Unit 31/56 O'Riordan Street, Alexandria, NSW 2015
First published in Great Britain in 2001
A PAPERBACK ORIGINAL
Text © Linda Newbery 2001
The right of Linda Newbery to be identified as the
author of this work has been asserted by her
in accordance with the Copyright,
Designs and Patents Act, 1988.
A CIP catalogue record for this book is
available from the British Library.
ISBN 1 84121 582 1
1 3 5 7 9 10 8 6 4 2
Printed in Great Britain

NO WAY BACK

Linda Newbery

ORCHARD BOOKS

For Sheila, Matthew and Alex
– at last!

The Swing Tree

From the beginning, Ellie resented Natalie. She was in the way.

Natalie appeared on the first morning of the autumn term when Ellie went as usual to meet Amanda at the corner of her road. There was a big chestnut tree there, with new conkers hanging in clusters, and some younger boys were throwing sticks up to knock them down. A year ago, Ellie would have joined in, and she would have done so now if no one else had been around. But Amanda was already there, and someone with her: a tall blonde girl.

'This is Natalie,' Amanda said. 'She's come to live in our road and she's in our year.'

Natalie and Ellie looked at each other. Ellie's first thought was that Amanda should have told her – they always walked to school together and home again afterwards, and they hadn't seen each other for nearly two weeks. Admittedly, though, Amanda hadn't had much chance to tell her; Ellie had only come home from France the day before yesterday. That was why she particularly wanted to walk to school with Amanda, just the two of them, the same as always. They had the last two weeks of holiday news to catch up on, but it wasn't going to be the same with Natalie there.

Natalie was taller than either of the others, and if Amanda hadn't already said that she was going to be in Year Nine, Ellie would have guessed that she was at least a year older. She stood leaning back against the street sign, resting on her elbows, one leg crossed over the other. She looked as if she'd been kept waiting long enough, and didn't see the point of hanging around for someone as insignificant as Ellie. She was pretty, with a small nose and a wide mouth, and blonde hair falling over one eye. Her skirt was short and her legs were long. She looked Ellie up and down, summing her up. Ellie felt as if she were the new girl, rather than Natalie.

'I bet you'll be in the same form as Ellie and me,' Amanda said to Natalie, 'because someone left at the end of last term.'

'Where did you live before?' Ellie asked.

'London,' Natalie said. 'My dad's got a new job, that's why we moved. He's always changing jobs.' She had a drawly way of talking, as if she threw her words carelessly aside to be picked up by anyone who wanted them.

'Hagley Heath must be *so* boring, when you're used to London,' Amanda said.

Natalie shrugged. 'I'll still see all my old friends.'

She didn't seem to expect to find any new friends worth having. Ellie wondered how she was going to keep in touch with friends as far away as London. There was a coach from Hagley Heath once a day, or you could go by train if you could afford it. Ellie hardly ever went to London – only for special occasions like family trips to the zoo or school outings to the Science Museum.

'Hagley Hall sounds posh,' Natalie remarked. 'Is it?'

Amanda laughed. ''Course not. Wait till you see it – it's just an ordinary comprehensive. It's called Hagley Hall because of the old house, but that's only the sixth-form centre.'

Hagley Hall School was on the edge of town, bordered by housing estates. Once, the Hall itself – a large, four-square Victorian house – would have been surrounded by its own farmland, but now it was swamped by housing estates. The ivy-clad Hall had kept its garden, where only the sixth form were allowed to go, and its high yew hedges, which shielded it from its noisy, sprawling neighbour, the main school. The newer buildings were of red brick, steel and plate-glass, with various extensions and mobile classrooms which seemed to have bred during the summer holidays. The walk from Ellie's house was quite a long one – a mile each way – but Mum said the exercise was good for her, and only took her by car in appalling weather. Ellie didn't mind, because she usually had Amanda to talk to, but now Natalie was going to spoil that.

All the way there, Amanda chattered away about which teachersNatalie would and wouldn't like, which subjects set most homework, which lessons were a laugh. Ellie might as well not have been there for all the notice either of them took of her. It was only when they were going in at the school gates that Amanda thought of asking, 'How was your holiday, Ellie?'

Ellie had been dying to tell her all about the Channel crossings, the rented flat in Normandy, the chateau they'd visited, the waiter who had misunderstood Dad's feeble French, but now she didn't feel like bothering.

'It was all right,' she said huffily.

In Ellie's opinion, the first day of the new school year was always a waste of time. They spent half the day doing nothing very much in their form-room – a mobile, this year, stuck between the library and the

Art block – and the other half having lessons with teachers who told them how hard they were going to have to work in Year Nine, with SATS tests and Option choices ahead, without actually giving them anything to do. It took a few days for things to get moving properly, but at least there was time to meet friends and to gossip about the holidays. Ellie's form had Mr Kershaw, who taught PE, for their tutor this year, and they could tell straight away that he wasn't going to be as strict as Miss Martindale had been in Year Eight. Miss Martindale had unfailingly checked whether newsletters had been delivered at home and had inspected everyone's uniform twice a week, hawk-eyed for unacceptable skirts, missing ties, multiple ear-studs, and other breaches of the rules. Mr Kershaw (Steve, as most of them called him except to his face) was young, track-suited and easy-going. As soon as he had called the register and handed out timetables, he wandered round the room, sitting on desks and chatting to people. Miss Martindale would have given them a pious thought for the day or told them to get into groups and share their views on starting a new school year.

At lunchtime, Amanda and Ellie and Natalie went outside with what remained in their sandwich boxes – like most people, they devoured two-thirds of their lunch during morning break. They sat on the grass between the main school and the Hall, and looked at the little Year Sevens in their spotless grey trousers and skirts, and red sweatshirts, carrying their new school bags importantly. Ellie reflected that only two years ago she had been like that, frightened by how big the school was and doubting that she'd ever learn her way around. Now, the Year Sevens looked and sounded like little kids and Ellie felt mature, an old hand, familiar with everything. The sunshine was warm and it would have been a relaxed, chatty lunch-break if she hadn't been so grumpy about Natalie.

'Those three boys who sit behind you – the ginger one and the tough-looking dumpy one and the dark one with the big nose – they're all idiots,' Amanda was telling Natalie. 'Jamie, Jason and Damien. They still think it's cool to flick bits of rubbers and stuff sweet wrappers down your back. But Steve Kershaw likes them 'cos they're good at football, and that's all a PE teacher cares about. Greg, the lanky one with glasses, is a bit of a weirdo – hardly ever speaks…'

She didn't seem to notice that Natalie wasn't much interested, looking across towards the path at a group of older boys.

'Greg's all right,' Ellie put in. 'He gets fed up with being picked on by Damien and Jason…' But neither Amanda nor Natalie took any notice of her.

'The black girl's called Lynette. She's OK, and so's

Jo – they're friends. Then the girl in the front row with the frizzy hair is Samantha Warburton. She's puke-makingly brilliant at everything.' Amanda seemed intent on working through the entire form. 'The one next to her with fair hair is Judith Sutherland. Ellie and I don't like her much. She's not nearly so brainy, but she's a real snob...'

Ellie picked moodily at a grass stem. She and Amanda had been friends since infant school; they always sat together and were in the same class for everything except French and Science. Besides, they spent a lot of their free time together, in particular at the riding school, where they helped out every Saturday. Ellie had never expected their friendship to be spoiled by someone else barging in. As the day went on, she was getting more and more fed up with the way Amanda treated Natalie. You'd have thought Natalie was royalty or a film star at the very least. Natalie didn't seem in the least surprised. Perhaps people always treated her like this.

Ellie gave up trying to join in. Starting to daydream, she was propped up on one elbow and gazing vaguely into space when she saw Luke in the distance, coming towards them along the path from the Hall. Suddenly, it became hard to swallow or even to breathe normally, and she concentrated hard on pretending nothing was happening. Seeing Luke always affected her this way. Sometimes Amanda teased her about it, but today she didn't even notice. Luke was in Year Thirteen now, and was wearing black jeans and the sixth-form black sweatshirt. Of course it was exactly the same as every other sixth-form boy wore, but Luke made it look as if he'd chosen it specially to suit him. He had a way of walking that Ellie could recognise anywhere – a quick alert walk, as if he were late for something, but she knew by now that he always walked like that, wherever he was going. He was small and compact compared to some of the lanky hulks in the sixth form, who trailed about as if walking at all were the most tremendous effort. Luke never trailed. There was an aliveness about him that Ellie found appealing.

When he saw Amanda and Ellie, he grinned and waved. Ellie liked that – lots of boys his age would think their younger sister and her friends were about as important as woodlice, and would walk past without so much as a glance.

Natalie waved back, although Luke wasn't waving at her. 'Who's that?' she asked, flicking her hair with a practised flourish.

'Oh, that's Luke,' Amanda said. 'My stepbrother.'

No one could have mistaken them for brother and sister. Luke was dark, Amanda fair; Amanda had a round smiley face while Luke's was thin and pointy. Elfin, Ellie's mum called him the first time she saw him. Ellie thought that was daft – it made her picture someone in green tights and tunic who lived in a toadstool – but Mum said it meant slightly-built, fine-boned. When Ellie told Amanda this, she pulled a face and said, 'Why can't *I* be elfin, then? It's not *fair*.' Amanda was – well, quite tubby, although Ellie's mum, who was nice about everyone, said that Amanda would soon grow out of it.

'He looks nice.' Natalie's eyes followed Luke as he walked away.

'Yeah, he's all right,' Amanda said. 'He helps me quite a lot with my homework.'

Ellie knew that Natalie hadn't meant that sort of *nice*. Ellie didn't like Natalie looking at Luke in that way – as if she was assessing him, giving him a rating. Ellie thought of Luke as her own private property, even though she knew it was stupid, because Luke was five years older than her and probably thought of her as a little kid, and besides he had a girlfriend his own age, Rachel Ashton. They'd been going out for a whole year. Ellie wondered why she didn't mind Luke going out with Rachel Ashton – she liked Rachel, who she sometimes met at Amanda's house – whereas she did mind Natalie noticing him. Amanda thought it was funny, Ellie liking Luke. A crush, she called it.

Ellie never thought of it as a crush, because a crush sounded like a silly schoolgirl thing, not serious, whereas Ellie was completely serious about Luke. She didn't mind whether he took any notice of her or not. It was part of his appeal, being so much older and so distant.

'*Step*-brother, did you say?' Natalie asked, still watching Luke, who had stopped to wait for two other boys cutting across the grass.

'Yeah, that's right.' Amanda brushed grass-mowings off her skirt. 'My mum married Bill when I was ten.'

'So you got a lush stepbrother as part of the deal? Not bad!'

Ellie, not liking the *lush*, said, 'New name, too. 'Manda used to be Byers, before. We were always next to each other in alphabetical order. It's Flynn now.'

Same as Luke. Luke Flynn. Ellie liked thinking the name to herself. She thought it would be nice to have an older brother or sister, instead of just Becky, who was five and starting today at the infant school. Being the oldest meant Ellie was always first – first to start school, first to take cycling proficiency, first to take the Year Nine exams which would be coming this year. When Amanda got to her GCSEs, she'd have the advantage of a brother who'd already done them, and got good grades.

A bell sounded from the building and people started moving back to their form-rooms, the Year Sevens jostling and running, the Year Nines and Tens sauntering, to show that they'd get there in their own time and weren't afraid to keep their form-tutors waiting.

It was Art all afternoon. Natalie sat with Amanda and Ellie, but in the middle of the lesson they were sent off to the Hall to have their photographs taken. Ellie hated posing for photographs. Mum said she'd look quite reasonable if only she could relax and behave normally, but Ellie couldn't help putting on a face that Mum said made her look like a constipated hamster. Dad would ask Mum how many constipated hamsters she'd seen and how she could tell what their problem was, but Ellie had to admit that Mum had a point. The photos had to be taken home in a cellophane pack so that parents could buy them and order extra copies, but Ellie always made her mum and dad send them back. She didn't want her sick hamster face looking at her from the mantelpiece.

They were lined up alphabetically for the photos. Natalie, whose surname was Bayliss, was in front of Ellie in the queue. She sat on the stool and threw her hair back and smiled like a supermodel posing for the front cover of *Elle*. Her photo would be lovely, Ellie could tell, and that made her come over even more hamsterish than usual when the photographer called out, 'Come on, you're next, aren't you? Elena Byrne!' Ellie raked her hands through her tangle of hair and sat down for her pose feeling stupid because everyone behind her in the alphabet was lined up watching. She couldn't help it – her face went all peculiar, the way it did after an injection at the dentist's, her mouth twisting itself into funny shapes. The photographer clucked at her, thinking she was messing about on purpose, and said, 'Come on, dear. I haven't got all day. Smile, it won't hurt.'

By the end of the afternoon, Ellie had worked herself into a state of resentment towards Natalie. She knew that it wasn't really Natalie's fault, but she just couldn't stop herself from being grumpy.

She went round to Amanda's on the way home, as she often did. Amanda asked Natalie to come too, but Natalie said she was going out later and was in a hurry.

'See you tomorrow then, same time,' Amanda called out as they parted.

'OK then. See you, Amanda. See you,' she added, glancing over her shoulder at Ellie. I bet she can't even remember my name, Ellie thought.

Amanda let herself in and they went through to the kitchen. Ellie loved Amanda's house. Amanda had lived in a flat in the town centre until her mum married Bill, and then they moved into the house where Bill and Luke had lived for years, since Luke's mother died. The house was older than Ellie's, which was on one of the new estates: it was bigger and more solid, with a proper hall and a stained-glass pattern on the front-door window. Ellie's house was just a box of red brick, with an entrance hall that was too small for two people to stand in at once and a little square of garden that had more paving slabs than grass. Here there was a big garden planted with shrubs and trees, and a swing tree at the far end, screened from the house by currant bushes. The swing part was Amanda's and Ellie's private place for talking when it was warm enough to be outside. There was even a pond with frogs and newts and dragonflies. And, of course, the added attraction that Luke might be around. It wasn't that Ellie hoped he'd come and talk to them in the garden; she was content with the chance of glimpsing him in the hall or kitchen, in passing.

They took home-made lemonade from the fridge and home-made biscuits from a cake tin (Amanda's mum was good at things like that; it wasn't surprising Amanda was plump) and took them out to the swing, followed by Joshua, the black-and-white cat. It was still sunny, with starlings chattering on the roof of the house and butterflies on the ice-plants, and the grass smelled warm when Ellie lay down on it. She was glad Natalie hadn't been able to join them. With just Amanda and herself and the cat, Ellie could pretend that nothing had changed. Or could have done, if Amanda hadn't wanted to carry on talking about Natalie.

'You weren't very nice to her,' Amanda accused, plonking herself on the swing. 'Not very *welcoming*.'

'Well, you made up for that.' Ellie's grumpy mood had left her since getting to Amanda's house, but now she felt it creeping back like a tide on the turn. 'You could have *told* me she was coming.'

'Didn't have much chance, did I? You were in France. Anyway,' Amanda went on, 'that doesn't explain why you've been in a right strop all day.'

'I didn't think it was that obvious,' Ellie mumbled.

'Well, it was.' Amanda was swinging, scuffing her feet on the patch of dried earth under the swing where the grass had worn away. 'You ought to have made more of an effort. Natalie's had a really terrible time.'

'Oh yes?' Ellie was curious, in spite of herself.

'There!' Amanda pounced. '*Now* you're interested. Typical! As soon as there's a hint of gossip you want to know all about it, after hardly speaking all day.'

'I suppose that means you're not going to tell me,' Ellie said. Joshua the cat came up to her, trilling, and then rolled over, wanting his tummy stroked. At least *he* wasn't being disdainful.

'I *will* tell you, just so's you'll have to stop being so horrible.' Amanda braked suddenly with both feet. 'Natalie's older brother was killed a year ago in a hit-and-run accident.'

'No, how awful!'

'And that's not all. Her mother's been practically an alcoholic ever since. That's really why they wanted to leave London – to get away from the place where it happened, and live where no one knows what happened, or about her mum being on the booze.'

Ellie stroked Joshua for a few moments while she took this in. Losing a brother like that must have been devastating (what if it had been *Luke*?) Natalie didn't exactly look grief-stricken, but then you couldn't expect her to spend a whole year doing nothing but weeping.

'Why did she tell you about it, then, if they moved away specially to keep it secret?' she asked.

Amanda gave her a pitying look. 'Honestly, Ellie, you are *dense* sometimes. Obviously she needs to confide in someone. That's not the same as broadcasting it to everyone she meets.'

'You shouldn't have told me, then, if it's secret! I didn't know,' Ellie said resentfully, 'that you and Natalie were such close friends, all of a sudden.'

Amanda looked suddenly doubtful. 'Well, she did say it was a touchy subject in their family, and not to tell everyone, only I didn't think that included you. Perhaps you'd better not mention it, all the same.' She looked at Ellie. 'I would have *thought*,' she added crushingly, 'that you could have said you were *sorry* for her, or how awful it must be for them. Instead of being jealous because I knew about it and you didn't.'

'I *am* sorry, and I'm not jealous,' Ellie said quickly.

She meant it – she really did feel bad about being unfriendly towards Natalie, who had to put up with being new at school on top of everything else. Tomorrow she would try harder, but meanwhile it was time to give Natalie a rest and talk about something else. She sat up and started twirling bits of dried grass for Joshua to pounce at. 'Have you seen that lovely new pony at the stables? Do you think we'll be allowed to ride it?'

Wasp

Looking round the form on Tuesday morning, Ellie thought that her class was an oddly-assorted bunch. Each year seemed to exaggerate the differences: when they'd all started together in Year Seven, it hadn't been so apparent. This year they were taught in ability groups for some subjects, like Maths and French, but for things like History and Geography and RE they were still taught as a form group. To Ellie, who was middling at school work, this didn't matter much, but at the far ends of the range there were people like Jamie Day, who was practically illiterate, in the same class as the real brains like Samantha Warburton and Greg Batt, who could probably have taken GCSEs this year without straining themselves. And then there were the physical extremes – lanky, gruff-voiced boys like Damien, and girls like Natalie who could pass for seventeen or eighteen out of school uniform, rubbing shoulders with tiny ones, like Scott. People shot up suddenly, she knew – she had grown about six centimetres herself in the last year, to the envy of Amanda, who remained short and dumpy – but at present Scott was small enough to seem like someone's infant brother underfoot, and it was difficult to imagine him ever being any bigger. Ellie didn't envy him on the sports field.

The class had a new teacher for History this year. Not just new to them or new to the school but *really* new, straight from training. With some teachers you couldn't tell, but with Mr Wishart it was obvious.

Ellie had often wondered why some people decided to be teachers when it was obvious they weren't cut out for it. Mr Wishart was one of those. Ellie had her suspicions from the minute she followed the rest of the class into the room and saw him standing uneasily by the front desk, looking as if he'd like to make a dash for the door while there was still time. He was tall and skinny and quite young, and he wore an obviously brand-new grey jacket that was a size too big for him, as if his mum had made him get the next size up so that he could grow into it. He looked as if he wasn't used to dressing smartly in a jacket and tie. He had well-cut dark hair and the sort of face that only just missed being good-looking. Ellie looked at him with interest, trying to work out why this was – something about his nervous expression, she decided. He looked as if he'd been dragged into the classroom to face thirty Year Nines like an early Christian thrown to the lions. His eyes darted nervously from one side of the room to the other, without actually looking at anyone. Jamie Day, whose ginger hair clashed horribly with his red sweatshirt, took one look at the new teacher and made a dash to the back row, followed by Damien Rogers and Eduardo Manelli and stocky Jason Read, who had shaved his head over the holiday and looked tougher than ever. They plonked their bags on their tables, sat with their chairs tilted back against the wall, and exchanged grins. Natalie said to Amanda, taking places in the row immediately in front of them, 'We'll have some fun with *him*.'

She didn't mean it in a nice way. Ellie looked anxiously at Amanda. Amanda was never awkward in lessons but Ellie had the feeling that Natalie might well turn out to be, given half a chance. And there were already enough troublemakers in the form to make life unpleasant for an indecisive teacher. Last year the class had been taught by Mrs Dar, the Head of History, who was small and quiet-voiced but could keep the class in perfect order without even appearing to try. History had been Ellie's favourite lesson last year, but she had the feeling that this might be a thing of the past. She cast a wary look at Nathan Fuller, the most volcanic person in the form, and was relieved to see him slumped on his desk looking completely dormant.

Mr Wishart stood in front of the class, fiddling nervously with a pen while everyone took a long time arguing about where to sit. He didn't tell them to hurry up, but just stood waiting, smiling tensely. At last he did a bit of *sshh*ing, and some of the more helpful people joined in until everyone was quiet. Then he said, 'My name's Mr Wishart and I'll be taking you for History this year.'

'Mr what? Did someone sneeze?' Jason said in the row behind Ellie, loudly enough for everyone near him to hear. There was a burst of laughter, and Mr Wishart glared at them and called out, 'Quiet, now,' but not as if he expected anyone to obey. He started to shuffle files and papers at his desk.

'Right then, I'll call the...er...register,' he said.

Ellie couldn't actually see the boys behind her exchanging conspiratorial looks but all the same she knew they were up to something.

'Er...put your hand up when I call your name, and then I can...er...see who you are,' Mr Wishart said.

The first two people on the register weren't likely to cause any trouble, but when he called out, 'Natalie Bayliss?' she replied, 'Yes, Mr Wizard.'

'*Wishart*,' Mr Wishart corrected her.

'Bless you,' Natalie said promptly. More laughter. Mr Wishart pretended not to notice, but he looked flustered as he carried on. 'Elena Byrne? Jo Cannon? Lynette Colburn?' He looked positively grateful to Ellie, Jo and Lynette for answering politely. 'Jamie Day?'

Jamie's hand flew up.'Yes…er…Mr…er…Wishart,' he mimicked.

'Matthew Eastwood?'

'Yes, Mr Vicious,' Matthew piped up in a silly voice, nearly choking with his own wit.

'Look here,' Mr Wishart said, with an attempt at sternness. 'This really isn't…er…good enough. "*Yes, sir*," will do. If people can't answer the register properly then we'll have to…er…stay in over break and do it then. Just put your hand up and answer "*Yes, sir*". Nathan Fuller?'

'Yeah,' Nathan droned, head buried in folded arms.

Ellie knew from the rustle of excitement that the boys behind her had something else in mind. From now on, each one answered his name politely, but when Mr Wishart looked to see who had spoken, someone else's hand would be up. At the end, Damien Rogers called out, 'You didn't call my name, sir.'

'Oh? What is it?'

'Darren Roberts, sir,' Damien said innocently.

'Darren…er…Roberts. Darren Roberts…' Mr

Wishart moved a finger down his class list. 'No, you're…er…not here. You'd better go and see Mrs Dar and find out whose class you're supposed to be in.'

'Yes, sir. Thank you, sir.'

Damien, smooth-skinned and blue-eyed, could look as angelic as a choirboy when he chose to. He went out, turning at the door with a cheeky grin at his mates. Mr Wishart seemed relieved to have the size of his class reduced by one.

'Er…right,' he announced. 'Here are your new exercise books. Could you give them out, er…?'

'Marvin,' said Matthew, who had had to sit near the front because all the back places were already filled. 'Yes, of course, Mr Wishart, sir.' He said it so smarmily that Ellie wouldn't have been surprised if he had bowed. He took the pile of books and started to fling them about, skimming them frisbee-style across the desks. The boys in the back row leaped out of their places like a Mexican wave. Ellie bent to pick up a book from the floor.

'No, no!' Mr Wishart shouted. 'Stop that!'

He had the kind of voice that went high and shrill when raised, no more authoritative than a duck quacking.

Matthew stood still, putting on an air of wounded good intention. 'I was only handing the books out, sir, like you said.'

'I said *hand* them out, not *hurl* them out,' Mr Wishart snapped. His face was flushed and he looked as if he'd rather be anywhere than here. Ellie felt sorry for him. He took the pile of books, told Matthew to sit down, and finished the handing-out himself. There were a few moments of relative order while everyone wrote names and form on the books. Mr Wishart returned to the front of the class and straightened his tie like a farmyard cockerel preening its feathers after coming off second-best in a scrap. Ellie hoped the fuss was over now. A token messing-about at the start of a lesson could be amusing, but it got tedious if it went on too long. She pulled a face at Amanda, which Amanda didn't see, but to her surprise the message was received and returned by Greg Batt in the row in front, who gave her an eyes-rolled-up *Can't we get on with it* look. Greg was a bit of an individual – far too bright, Ellie thought, to get involved in the time-wasting that was relished by the other boys.

'Right, then,' Mr Wishart began. 'This term we'll be looking at –'

He was interrupted by a screech from Natalie which made Ellie bounce in her seat with shock. Natalie sprang to her feet, flapping her book wildly and clattering her seat against Amanda's. Everyone looked round at the new commotion.

'*Now* what?' Mr Wishart asked wearily.

'*Wasp!*' Natalie shrieked.

Several of the boys jumped up too, swatting wildly with rolled-up exercise books, to show their appreciation of Natalie's potential as a new member of the Disruption Squad.

'All right, all *right*, everyone,' Mr Wishart yelled. 'Sit down. It's…er…only a wasp. No need for panic.'

'Don't worry, sir. I'll mash it,' Jason offered.

'No one's going to mash anything. Stay calm. Really I…er…'

'Urgghhh!' Natalie ducked as the wasp swooped close to her head, then ran to the corner of the classroom near the bookshelves. 'Keep that thing away from me! I can't stand wasps—'

Ellie looked at her in amazement and then at Amanda, who wasn't joining in but was laughing at the new interruption. Natalie had been fairly quiet up till now, nothing like this – playing along with the silly boys. From the way Natalie had acted yesterday, Ellie would have expected her to regard them as imbeciles, their antics beneath her, but now she was making all this amazing fuss. It was only a *wasp*, not a tarantula or a plague of locusts…

'Usher it towards the window, someone.' Mr Wishart was dancing about in the aisle between the desks, waving his arms. 'It'll soon fly out –'

'Ooh, usher it, usher it – I'm ushering, sir, look!' yelled Matthew, with camp gestures. 'Come on, Jace, *usher* it—'

'What's all the noise about?' Nathan asked irritably, rousing himself from his slump for long enough to look.

There was a scrum at the back and a triumphant '*Got* it!' as Jason sprawled full-length along the row of desks. The others looked disappointed as he examined the squashed corpse on his new exercise book and showed it to the boy nearest him, leaning across Jo Cannon to do so.

'Did you *have* to?' shouted Jo, who was always standing up for individual rights, whether human or animal. She didn't usually make a fuss in lessons but now she looked at the crushed insect and then accusingly at Jason. 'You vicious pig! There was no need to *kill* it!'

'It's only a wasp, stupid,' Jason jeered.

Jo squared up to him, chin jutting. 'Wasps have their place, the same as you do. You shouldn't interfere with the ecosystem.'

'What, by killing one wasp? Expect me to sit quietly and get stung, stupid?'

'Has it gone? Has he really killed it?' Natalie was still cowering in the corner with her hands over her eyes.

'All right, everyone, back to your...er...places. I

said, back to your places,' Mr Wishart shouted helplessly.

At that moment the door opened and Mrs Dar came in.

The usual thing happened. The class went from uproar to perfect order in two seconds flat. Mrs Dar stood in the doorway, saying nothing at all, with Damien Rogers smirking behind her. The boys melted into their seats and sat there as silently as stuffed dummies. Jo stopped threatening Jason with extinction and sat down meekly. Books were surreptitiously picked up off the floor and laid neatly on desks. You didn't mess with Mrs Dar. Natalie had never seen her before, but she took her cue from the others and slunk back to her table. She replaced her fallen chair and slid into it in one silent movement, and arranged her pens and pencils neatly beside her new book.

Mrs Dar still made no comment, although Ellie could tell from her quick eyes flicking around the room that she had her suspicions. Then she said smoothly, 'Mr Wishart, this boy *is* in your group. Surely his name was on the list I gave you? Damien Rogers.'

Mr Wishart checked his register and flushed bright red. He stared at Damien. 'I thought you said you were – er – Darren someone.'

'No, sir, I didn't.' Damien gazed back at him with

innocent blue eyes. 'I asked whether Darren Roberts was in this class, because I was going to tell you he's moved forms. You must have got mixed up.'

'No, I'm sure you told me *your* name was Darren Roberts.'

'Well, it isn't, so why would I say it was?'

'It seems there's been a misunderstanding.' Mrs Dar's glance swept over the class. 'Is everything else all right, Mr Wishart?'

'Er...yes. Er...fine, thank you, Mrs Dar.' Mr Wishart pushed a hand through his hair, making it stand out as if an electric current had been passed through him. 'I'm...er...we're...just about ready to start now.'

'At the end of the lesson, send me the names of any troublemakers.' Mrs Dar glanced significantly at Damien and then at Jason. She closed the door as she went out and everyone listened as her footsteps clopped away down the corridor. The force of her presence stayed with the class for a few moments, keeping everyone subdued. Mr Wishart took advantage by announcing, 'Right...er...we're going to be studying the First World War. Have a look at this sheet I'm going to...er...hand out.'

Ellie was glad that the lesson was going to start properly at last. Mr Wishart began talking about the reasons why the First World War was called the Great

War; it was clear that he knew a great deal about his subject and Ellie would have found it interesting if she hadn't had to strain her ears above the noise of chatter and fidgeting around her. Mrs Dar would never permit so much as a whisper to interrupt her, but as long as people weren't actually shouting out or fighting each other, Mr Wishart didn't seem to mind. When he set homework at the end of the lesson there were loud grumbles and groans. The moment the bell went, half the class stampeded out of the room without waiting to be dismissed. Judith Sutherland and Samantha Warburton, who always sat in the front row and worked hard whatever the lesson, followed more slowly, looking as if they'd been forced to spend a morning in a kindergarten.

'Er...you!' Mr Wishart pointed at Natalie. 'Wait behind.' Natalie stared open-mouthed and then swung round to the empty desks behind, as if there must be some mistake. 'Who, me?'

'Yes, you,' Mr Wishart said curtly.

'Unfair, or what?' Natalie complained. She slung her bag over her shoulder and walked as slowly as she could to the front of the class, exaggeratedly tripping over a chair which had been knocked over in the scramble for the door. Amanda and Ellie looked at each other.

'I'm waiting for Natalie,' Amanda said. 'I don't

know about you. This is out of order.'

Ellie wasn't going to be left out. 'Me too.'

'You two, wait outside the classroom, would you.' It was an order, not a question. Mr Wishart sounded far more confident now that he had three people to deal with instead of thirty.

Amanda humphed her way out, and Ellie followed. Outside, Amanda stood with her face pressed against the glass panel in a way which Mrs Dar would never have allowed. 'This isn't fair,' she grumbled. 'He's just picking on her 'cos she's new.'

'He's new himself, so how would he know she was?' Ellie argued. 'And she did make all that fuss about the wasp.'

'Oh, yeah? And what about all those boys telling him the wrong names? He hasn't kept *them* behind, has he?'

Amanda wasn't usually like this. She and Ellie usually sat together, working quietly, gossiping rather a lot but not actually causing any trouble. Now Amanda was beginning to sound like Natalie. Ellie felt uneasy. She didn't enjoy lessons like that.

After a few moments, Natalie stomped out and slammed the door hard. Ellie glanced back through the glass. Alone in the classroom, still red in the face, Mr Wishart was picking up the fallen chairs.

'He's well out of order, he is.' Natalie was furious.

'Picking on me like that. I told him I can't stand wasps and I'm allergic to them. He accused me of making it up.'

'Are you really allergic?' Ellie asked, a little suspiciously.

Natalie glared at her. ''Course I am. You think I'm making it up as well? Last time I got stung, my arm swelled up like a football and I ended up in hospital.'

'I expect he had to tell *someone* off,' Ellie suggested. 'We did give him quite a hard time.'

'That's his hard luck, isn't it?' Natalie said belligerently. 'He's a teacher, isn't he? He ought to be able to control us. It's what he's paid to do.'

'If you ask me, he picked on you just because you're a girl.' Amanda made a face through the glass panel. 'Didn't keep any of those moronic boys behind, did he? Not even Damien Rogers, and he made out he was someone else.'

In the classroom, Mr Wishart was sorting out the books and papers on his desk. Ellie wondered whether he was delaying leaving the room because Natalie, she and Amanda were still outside the door. Most teachers darted off to the staff-room for coffee as soon as the bell went for break.

'Come on,' she said. 'Let's go outside. That's taken up half of break as it is.'

Natalie was still complaining. 'I'm going to get my

mum up here to sort him out if he has another go at me. I'm not being picked on by a nerd like that.'

That evening, Ellie sat in the kitchen doing her History homework while Mum ironed. The kitchen was warm, full of the smells of hot shirts and shepherd's pie, and the iron hissed and thudded as Mum worked her way energetically through a basketful of washing. She claimed to hate ironing, although she always bashed through it cheerfully enough. If Ellie tried to do her own, Mum would watch for a minute or two and then say, 'Here, let me do it. I'll get it done in half the time,' as if she couldn't bear to watch someone else's clumsy hands at work.

Ellie was trying to label the countries on a map of Europe before the First World War. She thought she could do it, but it had been the wasp rather than the First World War that had dominated the lesson. Doing her homework was a sort of household ritual. Mum and Dad didn't go through her homework diary and check that she'd done it all, the way some people's parents did; it was more a matter of making space and time for it. Ellie didn't have a desk in her bedroom, which was too small to contain more than the bed and a built-in wardrobe, but she did have access rights to the kitchen table, usually while Mum was cooking. It fitted into the pattern of the evening, like Dad coming home from work, *The Archers* on the radio, Becky's bedtime, and Mum's evening class every Thursday. Usually everyone cleared respectfully out of Ellie's way, but today she might as well have waited until *after* Becky's bedtime. It was lucky she was only colouring in Austria–Hungary on the map at the moment, because Becky had started to learn the recorder and was in the lounge blasting tunelessly on one note. If you could call it a note – it was more like a banshee wail, shrilling in Ellie's ears and making her grit her teeth.

'*Mum.*' Her pencil was poised over Russia. 'Couldn't Becky go upstairs and play that? I'm trying to *think*.'

It came out more peevishly than she intended.

'Have you got a lot to do?' Mum draped the last shirt over a hanger and unplugged the iron.

'Yes, loads,' Ellie said, although she only had to finish this and then learn some French vocabulary.

Mum paused in the doorway with her armful of ironed shirts. 'Bad day at school?'

'Oh, it was all right,' Ellie said.

Usually she told Mum about the lessons she'd had or about anything special that had happened, but she didn't feel like it today. Perhaps it was childish anyway, to tell your parents everything. Mum stood for a moment in the doorway, expecting more, and then when Ellie picked up a blue pencil for Switzerland she went through to the lounge to remove Becky or the recorder or both. Ellie heard their cheerful voices going up the stairs, Mum encouraging, Becky exclaiming over something. Suddenly, she felt mean. And left out – but whose fault was that?

Birthday Present

'It beats me, what fun you two get mucking out stables all day long,' Dad said in the car on Saturday morning. He usually drove them to the riding school, which was five miles out of town on an infrequent bus route.

'Oh, Dad, you always say that,' Ellie said. 'And anyway I've *told* you. It isn't just mucking out. We do all sorts of things.'

'I shouldn't complain, I suppose.' Dad indicated right and turned into Amanda's road. 'There are far worse things you could be getting up to at your age.'

Visions of drugs, raves and wild parties floated into Ellie's head like streamers. She supposed that must be what he meant, though she had no intention of getting up to any of them, nor the opportunity, for that matter. For a moment he sounded like Aunt Belinda, Mum's much older sister, who seemed to imagine that Ellie would promptly turn into a teenage rebel on her thirteenth birthday, which had happened at the beginning of the summer holidays. All the relations she had seen since had mentioned her new teenage status: you're growing up fast, turning into a proper young lady, soon have the boys flocking round, and various other annoying things that grown-ups said to embarrass you.

Dad pulled up outside Amanda's house. Amanda scuttled down her front path, plump in black jodhpurs and a green riding-school sweatshirt, clutching her hard hat and a bag with her lunch in it. She looked so much like the old Amanda that Ellie felt cheered. At least this was one day of the week when they could be together without Natalie. She had tried to be pleasant, she really had, but Natalie didn't make it easy. She obviously didn't need Ellie as a friend.

Amanda slid breathlessly into the back seat and fastened her safety belt. 'I asked Natalie if she wanted to come,' she told Ellie. 'Did you know she used to go riding, where she lived before?'

'What, in London?'

'You can go riding in London. In Hyde Park and that.'

'Costs an arm and a leg, I bet,' Dad said.

'So is she coming, then?' Ellie asked flatly.

'Not today,' Amanda said, much to her relief. 'She

was going out, but she said perhaps next week. I bet she's a good rider, don't you?'

Oh, of course she would be, Ellie thought sourly. As far as Amanda was concerned, everything Natalie did had to be marvellous. It had never occurred to Ellie that Natalie might be interested in horses. If so, even Saturdays wouldn't be the same any more.

'Who's this Natalie?' asked Dad, who liked to be kept informed.

'Our new friend at school,' Amanda said promptly. 'Hasn't Ellie told you about her?'

'I think I might have mentioned her,' Ellie mumbled, although she hadn't. Dad glanced at her and she knew that the whole situation was clear to him, with no need for anyone to explain. He was good at picking things up. This could be comforting, but sometimes he saw things which Ellie would have preferred to keep hidden. To her relief, he said no more about Natalie, instead chatting to Amanda about her summer holiday until they arrived at the stables.

Larkshill Farm had recently been taken over by new owners, who had spent enormous amounts of money on upgrading it to Larkshill Equitation Centre and moving it upmarket. The cost of rides had gone up to match the new slickness and smartness, so that there was no question of Ellie being able to afford more than her one hour a week. The instructors – formidable Frances and friendly Paula – had been kept on. Ellie and Amanda, faithful regulars, helped out on Saturdays and sometimes in the holidays in return for the occasional free ride or extra lesson.

Riding Lessons. Liveries taken. Quality horses and ponies for sale, the new sign said. *Training for all types of competition.* Under Mrs Charwelton's ownership, Larkhill Farm had had no pretensions to being anything grander than a riding school for children. Nigel and Sue Hunt, the new owners, were young and wealthy, with a Range Rover, a point-to-point horse each, and confident loud voices. Amanda and Ellie had watched the changes with interest, and in Ellie's case not altogether with approval. She had liked dotty Mrs Charwelton who sometimes came out into the yard with her slippers on or forgot what day of the week it was. Now the stable doors were newly painted dark green, a burglar alarm system was installed, there were flower-tubs and hanging baskets around the yard and there was a big horse-box with *Larkshill Equitation Centre* painted on the sides and above the cab. It was rumoured that the Hunts had spent a fortune on turning the inside of Mrs Charwelton's comfortable doggy old house into something streamlined and modern, although Ellie had never been behind the belt of conifers which screened it from the yard to see for herself.

She always looked forward to Saturdays with the horses. The riding school had its own kind of order, its own routines; everything had to be done properly. The Hunts were too important to concern themselves much with mere Saturday helpers, and Frances, the Head Girl, was bossy and brisk, but Paula was much nicer and treated the girls as responsible members of the stable staff. Ellie liked that – the feeling that she was capable enough to be trusted with horses.

After their ten o'clock lesson, Amanda and Ellie would spend the rest of the day grooming the ponies, cleaning tack and sometimes helping Paula or Frances with a lesson, especially if there were young children or beginners who needed extra help. It certainly wasn't mucking out stables all day, as Dad thought – the Hunts were very strict about tidying up every pitchfork and wheelbarrow and stray wisp of straw before the first customer arrived. But then Dad knew nothing whatsoever about horses. If he passed a group of riders on the road he always eyed the horses with suspicion, as if fearing they'd attack his car with bared teeth and flying hooves.

Today, Ellie was eager to see the lovely grey pony that had arrived just before she went on holiday to France. She had seen Paula riding it in the paddock and it was the sort of pony she fantasised about: dark grey with a lighter mane and tail, very eye-catching, with a calm, contained energy that was released into floating elegance when Paula let it move up through its paces. The riding school ponies looked hairy and plodding by comparison. Its name was Florian, Paula had said. As soon as Dad had driven off, Ellie rushed to the list outside the tack-room hoping that she had been allocated Florian to ride, but beside her name it said *Seamus*, as usual. She was disappointed. Seamus was a nice pony and she was fond of him, but Florian was in a different league altogether. She could see him looking over a stable door in the livery part of the yard, throwing up his head restlessly, as if he'd have liked to be ridden.

'He's been sold,' Paula said later, when Ellie asked about him. 'He's staying on here though, as a livery. He's been bought for a girl about your age. A surprise birthday present.'

Oh, the lucky *thing*, whoever she is, Ellie thought enviously! She'd had a pair of jeans and a T-shirt for her own birthday. The thought of Mum and Dad announcing, 'We've bought you a pony!' was beyond the realms of possibility. She couldn't begin to imagine what a pony like Florian would cost, let alone how much the Hunts charged for full livery, or how much you'd have to pay for shoeing and vet's bills and all the other things that went with owning a pony. The expense was so overwhelming that there was no point even thinking about it. It would never happen to her.

All day, she kept thinking about the grey pony, sneaking along to the livery yard to look at him, until Amanda said teasingly while they were cleaning tack, 'It's a good job Luke doesn't know. He might be a bit miffed about being replaced by a pony.'

'He isn't replaced,' Ellie said quickly, feeling herself going red. 'Amanda, you haven't *told* him, have you? I mean, you know...'

''Course I haven't, stupid.' Amanda dipped a sponge into the bucket. 'Mind you, I don't need to. He could hardly miss the way you go all moon-faced and soppy when he's around. Just the same as you look now over that pony.'

Ellie flicked tepid water at her. 'I was just thinking that if I was that girl and Florian was *my* birthday present, I'd have been up here first thing, to do everything for him myself. There's no sign of her yet and it's nearly lunchtime.'

'You don't pay for full livery and then do everything yourself,' Amanda pointed out. 'That'd be pointless.'

'No, but surely that's part of having a pony. You wouldn't want to just turn up and ride it. That'd be no different from riding Seamus once a week.'

They finished buckling the bridles together and hung them on pegs with the ponies' names on them. Ellie liked cleaning tack; she liked the smell of leather and saddle-soap, and it was satisfying to see the shining tack ready for use. It would soon be greasy and dirty again, but she didn't mind that. It was lunchtime, and she and Amanda took out their Tupperware boxes.

Amanda yawned and stretched, looking suddenly gloomy. 'Why do we do it – work all these hours getting dirty and smelly? There's lots of other things we could be doing on a Saturday. Natalie's going to London, to someone's party.'

Ellie ignored the reference to Natalie. At the stables, she had thought, it would be possible to get away from her, but Amanda had kept mentioning her all morning: Natalie said this, Natalie thinks that. 'What's the matter?' she asked. 'You've never complained before.'

Amanda pulled a wry face. 'At least you're getting another ride this afternoon. I've got to help Frances with the tiny tots. I'm fed up with sorting out their stirrups and dragging ponies round and round. It's practically slave labour, the hours we work, for nothing. I'm not getting an extra ride today – it's not *fair*.'

She sounded so fed up that Ellie almost offered to

swap. She was due to go out on a hack as an extra escort, bringing up the rear to make sure no one got left behind or otherwise into trouble. It was certainly more fun than trudging round the indoor school with the small ponies. But Ellie couldn't really bring herself to give up the ride, and in any case Frances got annoyed if people interfered with her arrangements. Amanda's complaining made her uneasy, though. 'All this pony-business is just a phase,' was one of Dad's favourite – and annoying – remarks. Ellie was sure it wasn't true in her own case, but Amanda's enthusiasm did seem to be waning. She hadn't come to the stables as much as Ellie during the holidays, and didn't seem particularly pleased to be back now.

While they were putting their lunch remnants away, a sleek grey estate car came into the yard and three people got out: a girl with fair hair in a pony-tail, and two adults. Amanda grabbed Ellie's arm.

'See that? Judith Sutherland! She's never been here before, has she?'

'I didn't even know she could ride,' Ellie remarked.

Amanda giggled. 'Perhaps she's one of my beginners.'

But a new idea had struck Ellie, confirmed as Judith and her parents headed in the direction of the livery yard. Judith was wearing navy jodhpurs and carried a crop and a hard hat covered with black silk.

'Hey!' Ellie exclaimed, stopping dead. 'I bet it's *her!*'

'What d'you mean, it's her? Weren't you listening, cloth-ears? That's what I just *said*.'

'No, I mean she's the one who's been bought Florian. He's her birthday present!'

Why this should make it seem worse than a stranger owning him, Ellie wasn't sure. Judith had all the luck – she was pretty in her superior way, good at lessons, and now she had Florian as well, if Ellie's guess was correct. It was more good fortune than one person deserved.

Amanda stood for a moment with her mouth open. 'What, Jude the Prude?' she said, recovering. 'You mean her parents have splashed out a couple of thousand pounds, or whatever a pony like that costs? Just for *Judith*?' But she quickly took a positive view. 'Perhaps she'll let us ride him.'

'Why should she? We hardly even speak to her at school. It'd look a bit obvious if we suddenly started being smarmy now, just because she's got that gorgeous pony.'

'Worth a try,' Amanda said.

'Well, I'm not going to ask. You can, if you like.'

Ellie got the ponies ready for Paula's two o'clock ride, helped the children with their girths and stirrups, and brought out Freddie, her own mount, cramming her mass of hair under her hard hat before mounting. The children were competent enough not to need much chivvying from the rear and she was able to enjoy riding through the woods in the warm September afternoon, with the hoof-trodden tracks stretching under the trees like invitations. They had a brisk canter along the woodland ride, and Paula let Ellie lead two of the more experienced riders over the line of jumps – only logs and branches, but still jumps. Freddie was a keen jumper and the children looked at Ellie with gratifying admiration as she rode back to them. She didn't think much about Judith or Florian until later, when she was filling the water buckets in the livery yard. When she got to Florian's stable, Judith was in there unsaddling her pony.

'Hi, Judith,' Ellie said brightly.

Judith looked round. To Ellie's surprise, her face turned slowly red, and she said awkwardly, 'I didn't know you worked here!'

'Every Saturday.' Ellie looked yearningly at Florian. 'You are *lucky*, Judith, getting a pony like him. He's lovely.'

Judith didn't answer. She plonked the saddle over the stable door. It was brand new, very expensive-looking, made of cushiony soft dark leather, and there was a royal-blue saddle cloth underneath with *JS* on it in scarlet letters, as if Judith were a famous show-jumper.

'He's such a gorgeous pony,' Ellie said again,

watching the pony as he pulled at his hay-net. She couldn't take her eyes off him.

'Yes, he is.' Judith didn't sound particularly enthusiastic, much to Ellie's amazement. Didn't she *realise* how incredibly lucky she was?

'Had a good ride?' Ellie asked.

'It was all right, thanks.' Judith turned back to Florian to unfasten his bridle. Ellie refilled the water bucket from the hose, put it in its corner and went on to the next box, not understanding at all. Honestly, you'd think Judith would be ecstatic, delirious, drunk with happiness! If it had been Ellie, she'd have been leaping around with joy, wanting to tell everyone all about her amazing luck. What a waste, giving a pony like that to someone who thought he was just *all right*! Perhaps Judith was putting on a posh manner because she was a livery-owner now whereas Ellie was just a stable-hand. So much for Amanda's idea of cadging free rides! But no, Ellie thought, it wasn't snootiness that had most struck her about Judith's manner. She seemed different from her school self. There, she was quiet and a little disapproving, keeping herself aloof from the yobbish element, but here she seemed *unhappy* – impossible though it seemed in the circumstances.

Frances, small, dark and imperious, was two stables further along, rugging up one of the livery horses. She glanced round at Ellie as she entered, and said, 'Tell Amanda to take Trojan into the school for half an hour's exercise, will you? Just walking, tell her.'

Trojan was a riding-school cob who was recovering from lameness. Amanda was going to get an extra ride after all, although she was hardly likely to be thrilled by the idea of plodding round the indoor school on her own.

'And this bed's not banked up enough. Bring another bale of straw,' Frances ordered Ellie, who pulled a face as she turned away. No *please* or *thank you*, not from Frances.

Once, when she'd complained about Frances' bossiness at home, Dad had asked her why she put up with it, week after week. The answer was obvious: Ellie put up with Frances so that she could spend time with the horses. She had a sudden vision of Frances in the classroom, barking out orders like an army sergeant-major. She giggled at the thought. Maybe Frances and Mr Wishart ought to swap jobs? Mr Wishart might not be any better with the horses than he was with Year Nine, but Frances would soon sort out those idiotic boys, no problem.

Detention

'Lend me your French homework, would you?' Natalie asked Ellie before registration on Monday morning. 'I haven't done mine yet.'

Ellie hesitated. If Natalie had asked her to *help* with the work, she would have agreed straight away, but there wasn't time for that; it was only ten minutes until the bell went. Casual though Mr Kershaw might be, he would certainly notice someone copying someone else's homework.

'Well, I don't know,' she said. It hadn't been a particularly easy homework – a translation, which had taken her forty-five minutes of concentrated effort yesterday evening.

'Oh, go on, Ellie. Don't be mean.' Amanda gave her a look which said *I thought you were going to be nice?* 'It's not Natalie's fault if she can't do it. I'd lend her my book if I was in your set.'

Ellie sat down in her place and rummaged slowly

through her bag. Natalie hadn't said she *couldn't* do the work, only that she *hadn't* done it, which sounded like not bothering. Natalie had had the whole weekend to do it, just the same as everyone else. However, Ellie didn't want to argue with Natalie, or with Amanda for that matter, so she got the book out and handed it over.

'You'd better change a few things, otherwise Ms Aronson is sure to notice,' she warned.

''Course I will. I'm not stupid.' Natalie sat down and started copying rapidly in her large rounded handwriting that looked like rows of knitting.

Later that day, Ellie wished she had made some sort of bargain. *You can copy my French if you don't play Mr Wishart up*, something like that. Natalie had worked up a real grudge against the new History teacher. It was amazing, Ellie thought, how widely Natalie's attitude and behaviour varied from one lesson to the next. In Drama, which she liked, she was enthusiastic and purposeful; everyone already knew that when she got up to act it would be worth watching, whether it was a improvisation or a rehearsed performance. In Maths, with strict Mr O'Shaughnessy, the Head of Department, she sat in such perfectly-behaved silence that he probably thought of her as a shy newcomer who needed more self-confidence. She didn't like PE but was reasonably capable, if she could be bothered; in Social and Vocational Studies, which was currently all about sex and contraceptives and made Ellie squirm with embarrassment, Natalie knew it all already and was scornful of the idea that anyone their age needed telling about it by a mere teacher, especially Mr Jennings, who was far too old in her opinion to have had any recent practical experience. In French she was resentful, in Science unco-operative, and in History plain disruptive.

Ellie was learning to dread History lessons, even though the work they were doing was actually quite interesting. Some of the boys and Natalie had turned baiting Mr Wishart into a blood sport, and he wasn't getting any better at coping with it.

It was worse than just playing up. Playing up could be quite good-natured, but there was nothing good-natured about this. Ellie, who took no part in it, could feel the hostility in the air like death rays beaming towards Mr Wishart. Standing defiantly at the front of the class like a badger confronting terriers, he would retaliate with a ferocious snap now and then but was ultimately helpless. Every lesson made it worse.

Natalie and the sillier boys, and sometimes Amanda, didn't even sit down when they entered the classroom, but stood about in groups, as if it were the middle of break. Only after repeated shouts from Mr Wishart would they grudgingly slump into their places, rummaging lengthily and noisily in their bags. *We'll start when we're ready, not before*, their actions signalled. Another teacher would have made a joke about it, hurrying them along, but Mr Wishart didn't have the knack or the willingness to be jolly. It was so easy for Natalie and the boys to get him flustered.

Today, Ellie entered the room with a sense of foreboding and looked warily at Natalie to see what sort of mood she was in. Natalie's favourite tactic was to sit brushing her hair instead of getting out her books. If Mr Wishart made a comment she would mumble something rude, loudly enough for him to know, but not loudly enough for him to pick out what she had actually said.

Mr Wishart glared at her a few times. When that had no effect, he said acidly, 'Hurry up now. This is a classroom, not a beauty salon.'

'Not a *salon*,' mimicked Eduardo, putting on a posh accent and a camp attitude.

'I'd like History if we had a decent teacher,' Natalie remarked to Amanda, still brushing.

'What did you say, Natalie?' Mr Wishart shouted.

Natalie had a way of looking at teachers as if they came from outer space. 'I was just saying,' she said with poisonous sweetness, 'how much I love History lessons.'

Cackles from the boys in the back row, Jason and Damien and Jamie. Any experienced teacher would have separated those boys straight away and moved them nearer to the front.

'Stupid berk,' Natalie said, in a low but quite audible voice.

That was too much even for Mr Wishart. He jabbed a quivering finger in Natalie's direction. 'Right! That's enough from you. Move your things up here and sit next to Judith.'

Natalie jutted her chin. 'I'm not moving. I'm staying here.'

She was going to make it into a confrontation. Ellie's heart sank. The lesson was getting off to an even worse start than usual.

'Natalie, I told you to move,' Mr Wishart repeated.

'Yes, I heard. But I'm not moving. Why should I?'

Mr Wishart hesitated. Wrong again, Ellie thought; at this point he should have sent for reinforcements in the shape of Mrs Dar or the Year Head. No one was allowed to defy a teacher in front of the class and get away with it. But he probably wasn't going to, because it would mean admitting that he couldn't handle the situation himself. His face had taken on the pink puffy look that the class knew well.

'Natalie, if you don't move, I'll…'

'Yeah?' Natalie's eyes glittered. 'What will you do?'

'I'm not offering you a choice of moving or not. I'm *telling* you.' Mr Wishart was trying to sound strict, but he only succeeded in sounding panic-stricken.

'Go on, Natalie, move,' Ellie murmured, but it was useless against the vibrations of encouragement coming from the stupid boys behind. If Natalie gave in now, it would mean losing face in front of them.

'Come on,' Mr Wishart said in a more cajoling tone. 'I've told you at least twice. Now come and sit here next to Judith.'

'I don't want to sit next to Judith,' Natalie said loudly. 'She's a snob.'

There were hoots of laughter – nasty, vindictive laughter. Judith, who always kept to herself, wasn't popular in the class. She didn't look round or respond, but she bent her head over her open book and Ellie could see that she had flushed scarlet to the tips of her ears, her face matching her sweatshirt. Ellie had no particular liking for Judith, especially after Saturday, but this wasn't fair.

'That's out of order,' Jo pointed out to Mr Wishart. 'Jude's not involved in this. She shouldn't have to put up with being insulted.'

Mr Wishart looked at her, startled. 'No, you're quite right. Natalie, you must apologise to Judith, and I've already wasted enough time telling you to move. I'm not asking you again.' He moved down the rows and stood close to Natalie's desk, as if by towering over her he could induce her to move. Natalie still shook her head, stubbornly. For a moment Ellie thought that Mr Wishart was going to grab her by her arm and pull her out of her seat. That would only lead to further trouble. Everyone knew that teachers weren't supposed to touch you.

'Give her one more chance, sir,' Amanda suggested. 'If she messes about again, then she'll move.'

Natalie, still looking defiant, showed no sign of agreeing to this compromise, but Mr Wishart clutched at the straw Amanda had offered him. 'All right, then. But I'm warning you, Natalie. Any more trouble and you'll definitely have to sit at the front.'

He turned away and went to the front of the class. He had backed down, and everyone knew it. He shuffled through the file on his desk as if he had forgotten what the lesson was supposed to be about, while Natalie grinned round at the boys behind. The interruption had taken so long that Nathan Fuller had taken out a motor sport magazine and was flicking through it. Samantha Warburton, who sat next to Judith in the front row and had been ready to start ten minutes ago, sighed pointedly and looked at her watch. For her, that was outright insubordination.

At last Mr Wishart pulled himself together and got started. The annoying thing for Ellie was that the subject he was covering, the First World War, was really engrossing. When he was allowed to concentrate on what he was saying, he was a different person: enthusiastic, knowledgeable. He made it come to life in a way that the textbooks never could: reading out poems and stories, talking about the Pals battalions and the way women and girls had done all sorts of jobs. A lot of the time, he didn't even have anything written down – he had it all in his head, all the facts and figures, all the anecdotes. Natalie continued to yawn and fidget, but even Damien and Jason were interested, in spite of their usual complaint that they weren't going to do History as an Option next year, so what was the point?

While Mr Wishart handed out worksheets, Ellie transported herself to 1914. She would be nearly old enough to leave school, with an older brother who looked like Luke and was eager to join the army. He'd probably get killed in the Battle of the Somme the year after next, by which time Ellie would be out at work at a munitions factory and would have to support the whole family, because their mother would have two or three younger children to look after and the father would have been disabled in a coal-mining accident. The telegram would come to say that the brother had been killed, and Mother would sniff bravely and say, 'At least he died a hero's death,' like the mother in the Siegfried Sassoon poem that Mr Wishart had just read out. But Ellie would know it wasn't true, because Luke (he'd have to be called Luke, she decided, as well as looking like him – she could picture him in uniform, all skinny and vulnerable and trying to be brave) would have sent her heart-rending letters which described the squalor and the hopelessness of the trenches, so she would be the only one to know that he had died in some forlorn battle, mown down by merciless machine-gun fire with twenty or thirty others. Tears sprang to her eyes as she thought about it, and then she thought that she could add even more romantic anguish to the story if she cast Luke as her boyfriend rather than her brother, or perhaps she'd have called him her sweetheart in those days. Of course she'd never, ever get over the loss...

A prod in the back from Eduardo's ruler brought her back to the present. She turned round to see what he wanted, but he was only being annoying. She mouthed 'Get off!' at him.

'Do pay attention, Ellie,' Mr Wishart said sharply. 'You'll need to concentrate on this.'

That wasn't fair! She knew Eduardo was laughing at her. Fancy getting told off just for glancing round *once*, after the flagrant disruptions all round! Mr

Wishart was only picking on her because he knew she wouldn't answer back. Amanda, to Ellie's annoyance, was smiling; it was rare for Ellie to get told off. Natalie hadn't even noticed, too engrossed in her pose of intense boredom, eyes closed, one hand propping up her chin. It occurred to Ellie that the story she had just been making up wasn't all that different from Natalie's real life – the loss of a brother, a tragically early death. Natalie had never mentioned it or even hinted at it, but perhaps it was the one thing which could explain her difficult behaviour. Ellie could easily have hated Natalie at times for the nasty things she said and the way she drew attention to herself in lessons, but when she remembered the dead brother she realised that she ought to make allowances. No wonder Natalie was bitter.

Giving half her attention to Mr Wishart's comments on the worksheet, she began to imagine what Natalie's brother would have been like. Tall, she thought, with Natalie's blond Swedish looks, and an athletic build like some of the sporty boys in the sixth form. Quite cheeky, probably, but he'd be able to get away with it by being good-humoured, and not minding when people teased him back. His name would be Rob or Ross or something like that, and he'd be very popular, especially with girls. All the girls in his year at school would have cried when he was killed, and the boys would have been sorry because he was in the football team and a good laugh. There was probably one special girl who still went to his grave and laid flowers there. Did Natalie? Ellie wondered whether she would ever dare to ask.

At lunchtime, which followed History, Natalie was so entertaining that she seemed a different person. It was too cold to go out today, so they sat at a table in the canteen with their packed lunches and cans of Coke. Natalie knew lots of jokes and she told them well, so that Amanda and Ellie and the two boys who sat with them were in stitches of laughter. Once or twice Ellie didn't understand the joke and had to pretend to laugh with the others, rather than admit she didn't get it.

Eduardo and Matthew tried to join in, with 'Have you heard the one about the Englishman and the Irishman at the football match?', but their jokes weren't as witty or as well-delivered as Natalie's. With her acting talent she could put on funny voices and use pauses for emphasis in a way that made everyone fall about when she got to the punchline. One of the dinner-ladies came over to the table looking suspicious, but she could hardly tell them off just for laughing.

Later in the week, Natalie asked to borrow Ellie's

French homework again. 'I can't get the hang of those irregular verbs,' she complained.

Ellie still wasn't happy about letting her work be copied. 'If you'd asked me yesterday, I could have helped you with it at lunchtime,' she pointed out.

Natalie bit her lip and looked down. 'I was going to do it last night, but we had an awful evening at home. Mum got herself into a right state.'

Ellie got out her book and handed it over without another word, feeling mean for hesitating. She felt sorry for Natalie. Of course it must be dreadful at home sometimes, with all the memories of her dead brother. It wasn't surprising that Natalie couldn't manage irregular verbs, when she had such a tragic family background. Ellie wondered whether Natalie meant that her mum had gone into an alcoholic state, or merely (merely!) been overcome with grief.

She didn't give the French work another thought until last lesson on Friday afternoon, when Ms Aronson handed the books back. Ms Aronson was young, attractive and friendly, but nobody's fool. Handing Ellie her book she said sharply, 'See me at the end of the lesson. Natalie, too.'

'What's that about?' Jo whispered. She and Ellie sat next to each other in French, because both Amanda and Lynette were in other groups.

Ellie sighed, and whispered back, 'I let Natalie copy

my homework. And she obviously copied it word for word, mistakes and all.'

'Idiot,' Jo said. Ellie thought she meant Natalie, but only as the lesson began did she realise that Jo could have meant *she* was the idiot, for giving Natalie her work to copy.

At the end, when the chairs were up on the desks and the cleaners beginning to emerge from wherever they came from, Natalie and Ellie found themselves staring at Ms Aronson's desk looking at the two exercise books. Identical mistakes were ringed round in red.

'Last time, I was prepared to treat it as coincidence,' Ms Aronson said crisply, 'but twice in one week, and it begins to look as if someone's copying from someone else. Well, who is it? Who did the copying?'

Natalie put on what Ellie thought of as her Mr Wishart face – chin jutting obstinately, eyes looking neither at Ms Aronson nor at the books but somewhere into the middle distance, like a martyr waiting for a tedious ordeal to be over. She wasn't going to own up. Ellie, on the other hand, felt herself going cochineal-pink, the picture of guilt.

Ms Aronson wasn't going to be kept hanging about. She put some papers into her smart briefcase and snapped it shut.

'Well, I'm not waiting here all weekend. If no one's going to come clean, you leave me no choice.

You're both in detention on Monday.' She looked at both girls, giving them a last chance. 'In any case, whoever did the work is just as much to blame as the one who copied. You ought to know better, the pair of you.'

Ellie looked at Natalie accusingly. This was really a bit much – Natalie could at least have the guts to say it was her fault, not Ellie's. Ellie watched resentfully as Ms Aronson reached into her desk drawer, took out two detention slips and filled them in rapidly. Next, the slips would have to be signed by the Head of Year, Mrs Reynolds, which would mean traipsing all over school to find her. And then Ellie would have to tell Mum and Dad, because they had to sign it, too. She'd had only one detention before in her whole school life, and that had been for forgetting her PE kit twice running.

'Thanks a lot!' she snapped at Natalie, as their footsteps echoed along the empty corridor towards Mrs Reynolds' office. 'You could have *said*.'

'Wouldn't have made any difference, would it?' Natalie said off-handedly. 'She said we were both as bad.'

'But you've got me into trouble! It's all your fault!'

Natalie tossed her hair back. 'What's a detention, anyway? Don't bother me. Probably won't turn up, anyway.'

'Well, it bothers me,' Ellie retorted. 'I'm not in the habit of getting them.'

'Miss Goody Two Shoes,' Natalie mocked.

Mrs Reynolds' office was locked, so they went upstairs to the staff-room in icy silence, listened to her weary reproaches and went to find Amanda, who was waiting impatiently outside the main entrance.

'Where on earth have you been? I'd nearly given up.'

'Got a detention, didn't we?' Natalie showed her the letter.

'We? *Both* of you?' Amanda looked at Ellie in disbelief, but one look was enough to stop her from asking further questions. Natalie said no more about it, either from an overdue sense of guilt at having got Ellie into trouble or because detentions were too commonplace to bother discussing.

Outside the Keymarket shop on the corner of Station Road, Natalie said she had to get some things for her mum. 'See you tomorrow, then,' she called out as they parted.

'But it's Saturday tomorrow,' Ellie pointed out to Amanda.

'Yes, I know. Natalie's coming to the stables with us.'

Oh, fine! Ellie kicked at fallen leaves as she left Amanda at the corner by the chestnut tree and made her way slowly along her own road. That was all she needed. Natalie would probably tell Frances where to get off or say something nasty to Judith. It wasn't *fair*. (She seemed to have been thinking that quite regularly over the last few days.) She and Amanda had *earned* their places at Larkshill by proving themselves responsible and reliable and doing all sorts of tedious smelly jobs; Natalie shouldn't expect to just turn up and be treated the same. And presumably she was expecting Ellie's dad to give her a lift, too. She could have *asked*, not just assumed.

Meanwhile, there was the inquisition over the detention letter to be endured. Thinking about this made Ellie trail her feet more and more slowly as she neared home. Mum and Dad would be disappointed with her. They didn't interfere too much with her school life, but they did expect her to be polite, to do her work on time and to stay out of trouble. They wouldn't understand why she had let Natalie copy her homework.

It would be different at Natalie's house. With the sorts of problems her family already had, a detention was hardly likely to cause a row. She could see it now. Mrs Bayliss would be a plump woman with blonde permed hair and smudged make-up. She'd be red-eyed from crying the night before, bleary from drinking gin in the afternoon. The place would be a tip because she'd never get around to doing any tidying-up. Natalie would say, in the little-girl voice she could produce when she needed it, 'Mum, I've got a detention, just because I couldn't do my homework! That Ms Aronson, she doesn't explain things and then she tells you off when you get it wrong. She's always picking on me, just 'cos I'm new.'

And then Natalie's mum would say, 'What? You're new to the school and she can't even be bothered to help you with your work? Right. I'm going up there to sort her out.'

Natalie was always threatening to get her mum or her dad up to the school to sort out Mr Wishart or any other teacher who told her off. Lots of people threatened that sort of thing all the time, but Ellie wouldn't have been in the least surprised if Natalie actually did it.

Allowances

'Mum's driving you this morning,' Dad said while Ellie was getting her breakfast on Saturday. 'She's getting Becky some new shoes, so she'll drop you off on the way.'

'OK,' Ellie said through a mouthful of muesli. Mum came into the kitchen at that point, leading Becky by the hand, so she added, 'Er...Mum. Natalie's coming with us.'

Mum's eyebrows lifted into her thick hair. She had lovely hair, wavy and wild like Ellie's, but Ellie's always looked a tangled mess whereas Mum's looked as if it was supposed to be like that.

'Natalie?' Mum said. 'The one who got you into trouble?'

'Mm.' Ellie carried on eating, determined not to show how she felt about Natalie coming to the stables. Out of the corner of her eye she saw Mum and Dad look at each other.

'I may be wrong,' Mum said, 'but from what you said yesterday I've got the impression that you don't much like this Natalie.'

'I never said so!'

Last night, explaining about the detention, Ellie had made up all sorts of excuses for Natalie: she was new to the school, she hadn't done much French, she didn't know how the teachers liked things done. Mum and Dad hadn't been as annoyed as she expected, but it never failed to amaze her how easily they saw through her pretences. Mum wanted to write a letter to Ms Aronson to explain, but Ellie had said she'd rather do the detention and avoid any more trouble. It wasn't that she'd *lied* to them, it was more a case of them hearing all the things she hadn't said.

'I gather it wasn't your idea for Natalie to come today?' Dad asked, standing by the work-top waiting for the kettle to boil. Relieved of his chauffeuring duties, he was about to settle down at the kitchen table with a mug of coffee and the newspaper.

'No, it was Amanda's.' Ellie gulped down the last spoonful and took her cereal bowl to the sink. 'I suppose Natalie's more her friend than mine, really.'

There, she'd as good as told them now. She felt left out. She was jealous. These weren't nice things to feel, and she didn't want them spilling over into her Saturday. 'We'll be late,' she said, looking at Becky, who wasn't even dressed yet; her hair was all tousled and she was still wearing her pink pyjamas with the teddy-bear on the front.

'No, we won't,' Mum said. 'It's only ten past.'

Becky clambered into the chair opposite Ellie's and demanded chocolate spread on her toast. Ellie looked at her enviously. She didn't usually envy Becky, but suddenly life seemed so beautifully simple for a five-year-old, uncluttered by problems and dilemmas. Becky had just started proper infants' school and had come home yesterday very proud of a gold star she had been awarded for a picture. A gold star for Becky, a detention for Ellie. Just now, Ellie would willingly have swopped her detention, jealousy and resentment in exchange for a gold star, chocolate spread and a visit to town with Mum for new shoes.

And she needn't even have mentioned Natalie, because when the car pulled up outside Amanda's house Amanda came out by herself, hurried and breathless as usual, sliding into the back seat beside Becky and strapping herself in.

'I thought Natalie was coming?' Ellie could only suppose that Natalie expected individual door-to-door service. That would be just like her.

'No, she's not coming till later. She's not riding, just coming for a look round,' Amanda explained.

Mum seemed a bit disappointed that she wasn't

going to see Natalie – Ellie knew she was curious about her. 'Perhaps it's just as well she's not on your ride, if she's only just starting to learn,' Mum said. She had been greatly impressed last time she had stayed to watch, when Ellie and Amanda had been jumping in the indoor school.

'Oh, she's not a *beginner*,' Amanda said, as if the idea were ridiculous. 'She's ridden a lot. She's probably better than us.'

At least I'll be spared having to admire her wonderful riding today, Ellie thought sourly. But surely, if Natalie were so experienced, she wouldn't want to hang round the stables the way Ellie and Amanda did, being bossed about by Frances and doing all the tedious yard jobs? It didn't strike Ellie as the sort of thing Natalie would enjoy in the least.

A good ride on Freddie put her in a better mood, especially as Paula had made a small course of jumps in the school and put them up higher just for Ellie and another girl after everyone else had gone round. Amanda, riding the stolid and sleepy cob Rosebay, looked on grudgingly. Rosebay would just about heave herself over the jumps, given a lot of hard work from her rider; there wasn't much excitement in riding her. Amanda hadn't been allowed to ride Freddie yet.

Leading Freddie back to his stable afterwards, Ellie half-regretted that Natalie hadn't been there to watch; he had jumped really well and she hadn't ridden badly, either. But when she came round to the tack-room with Freddie's saddle and bridle, she found Natalie standing there. She was wearing black jeans, high-heeled boots and a clingy white sweater, and was looking over the half-door at Spanish Ledge, Nigel Hunt's event horse.

'Hello,' Ellie said, because she had to walk right past Natalie to get into the tack-room.

'Oh, hello,' Natalie said. She seemed different away from school – almost shy. 'This is a big one, isn't it?'

'His name's Spanish Ledge,' Ellie said, pausing to look too because Spanish Ledge was so beautiful, a bay thoroughbred whose coat shone with health and grooming. He looked round at them, chewing a mouthful of hay. 'He's an event horse,' Ellie said. 'Nigel – that's his owner – wants to qualify him for Badminton in the spring.'

'Oh, is he a real show-jumper?'

Ellie looked at her curiously. There was something odd about this. First, Natalie's clothes – not very practical, those smart boots and a white sweater that was bound to get filthy – and second, everyone knew that Badminton was a three-day-event, not show-jumping. Her doubts increased when Amanda appeared and they both took Natalie to the pony yard.

'I like that black-and-white one,' Natalie said,

pointing to piebald Piccolo. It was becoming obvious that she knew practically nothing about horses – even less than Ellie's dad, and that was saying something. Amanda must have realised, too, but Ellie didn't dare to look at her. When she thought of Natalie making it all up, pretending she'd done lots of riding, she realised that Natalie wanted to fit in, to be like Amanda and herself. To her surprise, she found herself warming to Natalie. Here, Natalie was the one who felt left out. She wanted to join in, to learn. It was a new side of her, and one which Ellie liked a lot better than the loud, arrogant side.

Frances had gone to a show today, but Paula was quite happy for Natalie to help out. All three girls went to fetch the ponies who were still out in the field and brush them off, and later they all cleaned tack together. Ellie noticed Natalie watching herself and Amanda, copying, not actually asking what to do, although Ellie had to put the bridles back together again. At one point Nigel Hunt poked his head round the door, smiled vaguely and went away again, without seeming to notice the extra person. Ellie had hardly ever spoken to him; he was over six-foot and his gaze rarely descended to her level, as if she were some lesser species scuttling around at his feet. He was good-looking in a lean thoroughbred way, dressed in cords, chunky sweater and a peaked cap.

'Who's that?' Natalie asked, going to the door to watch as Nigel walked on towards the house. 'He's all right, isn't he?'

Amanda giggled. 'That's Nigel. He owns the whole place. And he's married, so you'd better not get interested.'

'Not bad, though. And must be loaded if he owns this place. What's his wife like, then?'

'Sort of the same. A female version,' Amanda said.

'And they're show-jumpers? Do they ever take you with them to the big shows?'

Amanda puffed out her cheeks, meaning *That'd be the day*. 'Not likely. Frances goes, or sometimes Paula as groom. We stay here to do all the dirty work.'

'Lunchtime,' Ellie said, hearing the clatter of hooves in the yard as the ponies from Paula's lesson came out of the indoor school. 'We've got to get the ponies unsaddled, then we can have our sandwiches.'

Natalie looked at her watch. 'I'm off now. I didn't bring any lunch and anyway I've got to meet someone. Why don't you come round though on your way home?' she added, looking at Amanda. 'My mum and dad are going out and I'll be on my own.'

'OK then. Shall we?' Amanda looked at Ellie, although Ellie wasn't at all sure she was included in the invitation. 'See you about half past five, then? Are you going to ride next week?'

Natalie looked doubtful. 'I might. If I can afford it.'

When they'd seen to the ponies, Ellie and Amanda took their lunch up to the top of the hay-bales and arranged loose hay into tickly sofas. Ellie was beginning to feel bad about the way she'd judged Natalie. It sounded as if Natalie really couldn't afford to come riding – well, it was expensive. Ellie's parents had been staggered when the Hunts had put the hourly rate up to eighteen pounds. Ellie and Amanda paid half-price in return for their stable work, but even so she knew it was a struggle for her parents to fork out once a week. She wondered whether Paula might arrange a free ride for Natalie if the situation were explained to her, in return for Natalie's help around the yard.

'It's all right for *Judith*,' she remarked, opening her lunchbox. 'She can ride as much as she wants, and she doesn't even seem to want to. Poor old Natalie can't afford it, from what she said.'

Amanda gave a triumphant smile. 'I knew you'd like Natalie in the end. She's been OK today, hasn't she? Aren't you sorry now that you were so mean?'

Ellie hesitated, still thinking about the detention. 'Well – she's so *different* here. Not the same person at all that she is at school. Nicer.'

'She's had a lot to put up with,' Amanda said with her mouth full. 'You have to make allowances.'

Ellie considered. 'Like people do for Nathan.'

Some people had such awful problems at home that she knew she ought never to complain about life being unfair – even when someone like Judith was dished out such an enormous slice of luck. Ellie knew that she was lucky herself, to have a nice mum and dad who cared for her and for each other, and a family that was in no danger she could see of falling apart. In her own class, there was Jo, whose parents had recently split up, with Jo shuttling backwards and forwards from one parent to the other so often that it hardly seemed worth unpacking her bag. Matthew lived in a leaky caravan with his dad and seemed to exist on chips and Coke; Sanjay had to put up with racist yobs yelling *'Paki'* at him in the street. And then there was Nathan Fuller, who was always in a foul mood whenever he'd spent the weekend with his father and would unfailingly pick a fight with the first teacher who spoke to him on Monday. Most of the staff knew how to deal with it and would give Nathan cooling-off time, but there were explosions if he came across a teacher who didn't know him.

'Remember that mouthful Nathan gave Mrs Reynolds when she did a uniform check?' Ellie said.

'Exactly. He didn't even get done for it, did he?' Amanda passed a bag of crisps. 'All he got was a friendly chat in her office afterwards. If it had been you or me we'd have been suspended, but they've got to make allowances, like I said.'

From where they sat, high above the yard, Ellie could see Judith's parents' charcoal-grey Audi pulling up in the yard, and Judith getting out. In spite of spending so much money on Florian, the parents couldn't even be bothered to get out of the car to look at him.

'There's nothing like the horse world for making you feel like a complete nobody, is there?' Ellie remarked. 'If you haven't got money to throw around, you might as well forget it.'

'That's what I was saying earlier,' Amanda said, 'about how they exploit us here. I mean, it's Us and Them, isn't it? There's rich people like the Hunts and Judith, who've got posh horses and go off to shows. Then there's slaves like us who'd do anything for a free ride.'

Ellie was so fixed on the idea of Natalie's family just about managing to scrape a living that she was astonished, after the bus journey home, when Amanda led the way up the drive of one of the smarter houses in Dorset Road. Ellie stopped in confusion.

'What are you going up here for?' she asked. She had imagined a boxy little place like her own family's. This looked palatial, the sort of house Ellie's parents had seen in estate agents' windows, sighed at and quickly passed over. Their chances of living in a house like this were about the same as Ellie's chance of owning a pony like Florian.

Amanda stared at her. 'It's where Natalie lives, gormless.'

'What, here? I thought—'

'Yeah? What did you think?' Amanda challenged her.

'Well, you know – not being able to afford to go riding – I thought she'd live in a tiny house like mine, or a council flat or something—'

But there weren't any little box houses in Dorset Road. Natalie's house was big and detached, one of the smart new ones that were meant to look Georgian. It had a shrubbery in front with the ground between the plants covered in wood-bark, and there was a double garage with a Volvo estate parked outside. Ellie tried to readjust her ideas once again while Amanda rang the bell and they waited in the glazed and tiled splendour of the porch.

'I expect she meant,' Amanda explained kindly, 'that she didn't *want* to spend eighteen pounds of her own money on riding. She gets an allowance – I don't mean just pocket money, a proper allowance for clothes and going out and everything.'

Ellie wasn't at all sure about being here; Natalie had only meant to invite Amanda. But Natalie opened the door without surprise and led the way up to her bedroom. Ellie had to try not to goggle too obviously.

Natalie's room was huge, with a sofa as well as a bed, and it had its own shower room adjoining. There was a TV and video on a swivel stand and there were floor-length curtains with a pelmet and tie-backs. It looked positively opulent to Ellie.

'I'll get some drinks,' Natalie said, and disappeared downstairs. There didn't seem to be anyone else at home. Thinking of the dead brother, Ellie sat on the sofa and scanned the pin-board for a possible photograph, but the only pictures were of recognisable film actors, footballers and rock groups. She was about to whisper a question about the brother to Amanda when she heard Natalie's feet on the stairs, and Natalie came back into the room with three cans of lager, which she handed out.

Ellie turned the chilled can in her hands, uncertain what to do. She'd tasted lager before but didn't much like it, and was sure she couldn't manage a whole can by herself, but Amanda opened hers, looking at Ellie with a *Go on then!* expression and she knew she was going to have to.

'I'm going out with Jonno and Sophie later,' Natalie said, 'but there's no rush.' She seemed different again, in charge, full of the confidence that had deserted her at the riding school. She sprawled on her bed and looked lazily at the other two. 'What do you two do for kicks then, when you're not hanging round the neddies?'

Ellie wasn't sure what to say. Going to the stables *was* what she did for kicks, as Natalie put it. Sometimes she and Amanda might go to the cinema together or to a disco, but she was sure that discos at the Youth Centre or occasionally at school weren't Natalie's idea of a good time. On Saturday evenings, if it was warm enough, Ellie's family sometimes had a barbecue in their tiny square of back garden and Dad would play his old seventies tapes – that was about the most exciting thing she could look forward to this evening.

'Nothing much,' Amanda said. 'It's so *boring* round here.'

'You ought to come out with me some time,' Natalie said, in the languid way she had, as if she didn't care much one way or the other. 'My mates are a great laugh.'

'Could we?' Amanda said eagerly.

Ellie sipped at her lager, feeling it bubbling into her nostrils, its bitter taste filling her nose and her mouth. She wasn't sure she wanted to go out with Natalie. Natalie always seemed two or three years older than herself and Amanda and she was sure the 'mates' would be the same. What would they do, where would they go? Ellie didn't feel ready yet for Natalie's mates. Saturday barbecues at home were a lot safer.

Judith

On Thursday lunchtime, when Ellie was changing her library books, she found herself waiting behind Greg Batt at the issue desk. He was in the middle of a complicated transaction involving a whole pile of books: returning some, renewing another, taking out two new ones and asking for something he'd heard reviewed on the radio. Ellie looked sideways at the pile to see what sort of thing he was reading. There was quite a mixture: computer-aided design, Arthurian legend, the origins of life and mathematical puzzles.

He saw Ellie looking and handed her the book he still had in his hand. 'You ought to try this – it's about the First World War. It's really good,' he said.

Ellie took the book and looked at its cover, and then at the blurb on the back. Mrs Abbot, the librarian, beamed approvingly. It was a novel by an author Ellie had never heard of, its cover showing a boy in soldier's uniform and a girl dressed as a nurse.

According to the blurb they were both eighteen, just old enough to take part in the war. Ellie liked the idea of a book about war that had a girl in it and wasn't just about men fighting.

'Thanks,' she said. 'I'll get it out then, if you've finished with it.'

Greg wore wire-rimmed glasses with the kind of lenses that made his eyes look enormous and swimmy underneath. He was an odd, serious boy, spending his spare time either alone or with Sanjay, devising projects of his own as well as his school work. The others in the class called him, predictably, Batman, or the Caped Crusader. When Mrs Abbot handed him the books he'd had issued, he hovered uncertainly for a moment as if he wasn't sure what to do next. Then he said quickly, 'I thought that story you read out in English was really terrific,' and pushed his way through the library turnstile.

'Well! There's a compliment,' Mrs Abbott said brightly, stamping two books for Ellie, the one she'd already chosen and the one Greg had given her.

Ellie felt herself blushing with pleasure and embarrassment. The story she had read out – or rather been *made* to read out; Mr Barrington didn't give you much choice – had been based on her daydream in the History lesson, the one about the soldier and the telegram. She'd had to change the soldier's name to John when she read it out, because otherwise both Amanda and Natalie would have teased her endlessly for being soppy about Luke. Amanda had said it was a good story and so had Mum and Dad, but then they'd probably felt obliged to say something nice. Greg didn't have to say anything at all, and Ellie felt that his praise was worth having; he read so widely and knew so much. She couldn't help smiling to herself, but as she walked back to the form-room she remembered that she was in a strop with Amanda, and adjusted her expression accordingly.

It was getting to be a habit, spending lunchtimes on her own: getting her homework done in the library, or just reading. Lately, she'd been choosing to disassociate herself from Natalie and Amanda, at least at lunchtimes. Natalie had a boyfriend now – Jonno, who had started in the sixth form but left after the first week. Although it was forbidden for outside friends to enter the school grounds, Jonno, who worked in a nearby garage, usually managed to sneak in at lunchtimes to see Natalie and some other friends. Amanda had started to tag along too, and Ellie suspected she was keen on a boy called Darren in Year Eleven. Not wanting to play gooseberry to the various pairings, Ellie stayed away. She felt hurt and martyred about it, but no one noticed. In fact, she was *deliberately* being a martyr, glooming about on her own, because she could easily have spent the time with Jo and Lynette if she'd wanted to. They were getting together a team for inter-form netball and were trying to organise some lunchtime practices, and although Ellie wasn't brilliant at netball she knew they'd have her in the team. Perhaps next week, she thought.

Amanda and Natalie were last to come in for registration, as usual. Mr Kershaw looked at his watch rather pointedly, but said nothing and marked them present.

'Did you get all your homework done, Ellie?' Natalie said in her patronising way as she sat down, taking a hairbrush from her bag.

Ellie didn't answer, but Greg Batt looked up, caught her eye briefly and then went back to his reading. She recognised a silent but sympathetic ally – she was sure Greg knew exactly what was going on.

Ellie hoped that Natalie would give up any ideas about coming to the stables, especially now that she'd seen how mundane the work was, but on Saturday she appeared when Ellie and Amanda had finished their ride.

'I want to see all the stables and all the horses,' she said.

'OK, we'll show you round,' Amanda offered.

Ellie really couldn't see what the attraction was for Natalie, but she followed, prepared to give her the benefit of the doubt if she really wanted to learn about horses. When they returned to the main yard they found Frances standing there, dressed ready to ride and holding her hard hat and dressage whip. Confronted by her disapproving glare, Amanda broke off her running commentary on all the horses and their personalities.

'Ellie, you're supposed to be raking the indoor school,' Frances said. 'Amanda, why aren't you helping Paula in the pony barn? And who's this?' Her sharp eyes swept Natalie up and down.

'Our friend, Natalie,' Amanda explained. 'She's come to help.'

Frances looked disparagingly at Natalie's unworkmanlike attire. 'You shouldn't bring friends here without asking,' she told Amanda, 'especially if it keeps you from your jobs. And you know perfectly well that all visitors must report to the office.' She forced a smile at Natalie, and added, 'If you want to book a riding lesson or a hack, then of course you'll be welcome. But we've got all the help we need at the moment. Amanda, Paula's waiting for you.'

She strode off in her shiny leather boots. Frances always strode: she never merely walked. Everything about her was purposeful, and she expected everyone else to be the same. Amanda stuck her tongue out at the booted and Barboured rear view.

'Who's Miss Bossy Boots then?' Recovering, Natalie assumed her classroom self, mouth twisting into an expression of amused dislike.

'That's the Head Girl,' Amanda explained. 'She runs the place and she's a bit of a pain. We like Paula better.'

'Head Girl? Sounds like one of those old-fashioned girls' boarding schools. She looks a right slave-driver. Does she always walk around with a whip in her hand? Work, work! Faster, faster!' She mimed beating galley slaves.

Amanda giggled. 'It's a dressage whip,' she said, and began to explain how you flicked it without taking your hand off the reins, but at that moment Frances reached Spanish Ledge's stable and turned round at the door to shout, 'Amanda! I've told you once! Don't stand about chatting when there's work to be done!'

'How much do they pay you, then, to order you about like that?' Natalie asked indignantly.

Amanda reddened. 'We don't actually get *paid*. We get our lessons half-price, and free rides instead. Sometimes.'

'You're kidding! And Miss Jackboots there's got the cheek to tell you off for spending two minutes talking! Who the hell does she think she is?'

Ellie didn't dare wait any longer, as Frances was pointedly standing with one hand on Spanish Ledge's door waiting to see whether they obeyed her instructions. Collecting a rake from the shed by the indoor school Ellie got on with her job, assuming that Natalie would leave. Frances could have been more pleasant, Ellie thought – she could at least have given Natalie the chance to do something useful. But on the other hand, Ellie knew that Natalie would never understand why she and Amanda chose to work here for nothing. It wasn't like working in Tesco's or doing a paper round; you didn't do it for money, but for the chance to work with horses and gain expertise. When time for work experience came in Year Eleven, Ellie was going to ask if she could come here for the week, even though Mum and Dad would no doubt want her to do something in business. She could hear Dad now: 'What, spend the whole week mucking out stables?'

It took a long time to flatten out the deep groove made in the peat by hooves treading a regular pattern around the edge of the school. Before she was a quarter of the way round, Amanda called her from the open door.

'What? You'll be in trouble if Frances sees you,' Ellie called back.

Amanda came in, the dust from the dried peat

settling on her rubber riding boots. 'No, I won't. I'm going.'

'What do you mean, going?' Ellie propped up her rake and leaned on the handle.

'I agree with Natalie. I'm fed up with being treated like a slave. Bossed about by Frances, expected to jump to it when she clicks her fingers. I've had enough of it. It's exploitation, that's what it is.'

There was something of Natalie in the way Amanda said it – the tilted chin, the hard-edged voice. Her eyes didn't meet Ellie's. Ellie could tell that it was partly Natalie speaking.

'Amanda! You can't just walk out!' she protested.

'Why can't I? I'm going into town with Natalie.'

'Leaving Frances and Paula in the lurch?'

'Serves Frances right, doesn't it?' Amanda traced a pattern in the raked peat with the toe of her boot. 'If she wants people to do things for her, she should at least be nice to them. The way she yelled at us just now was well out of order.'

Ellie's fingers gripped the handle of the rake as if by holding tight to it she could stop her stable Saturdays from slipping away.

'You can come too if you like,' Amanda offered. 'That'd really show them.'

'No, I'm staying,' Ellie said. It wouldn't be the same without Amanda but she still couldn't give up all contact with the horses, just on a whim. 'Have you told Frances?'

'No.' Amanda looked uneasy. 'You can tell her if you like, when I've gone.'

'Oh, can I? Thanks a lot!' Ellie began raking again, with quick angry swipes that scattered dust over her own and Amanda's boots. 'That's a bit much. Anyone would think you were scared to tell her.'

'I'm not,' Amanda said, not very convincingly. 'But I like the idea of just disappearing. It's a way of making my point. She shouldn't take me for granted.'

'What's the big attraction of going into town, anyway?' Ellie asked, still raking. Going into town was something you could do any day of the week, after school.

'Oh, you know,' Amanda said vaguely. 'Meet Natalie's friends, go to the record shop, try on clothes, that sort of thing.'

'When you could be—' Ellie had been about to say, 'When you could be riding Trojan?' but she stopped, realising that all the things they normally regarded as privileges – being entrusted with a child beginner, escorting a ride, exercising a convalescent pony – had suddenly lost their appeal for Amanda. Amanda was fed up with hard work and clothes that smelled of horse sweat. She wanted to hang around with Natalie and those boys. Drat Frances, Ellie thought: if she'd been nicer to Natalie, this wouldn't have happened. Not yet, anyway. She was beginning to realise that it was inevitable, sooner or later.

'I said you could come too,' Amanda repeated, 'so you don't have to go all huffy.'

Ellie shook her head. 'What about our Saturday morning rides? You're not going to stop riding altogether?'

'Oh no, I've already booked for next week,' Amanda said. 'But I'm not helping out any more. There are better things to do than shovel manure.'

Ellie could see how it would develop. Before long, Amanda would think Ellie was still stuck in a childish pony-phase, the way Dad said.

'Well, bye then,' Amanda said. 'I'll see you on Monday.'

'Bye.' Ellie didn't look up. She felt too annoyed with Amanda, annoyed with Natalie, annoyed with everything.

It didn't take long for Amanda's defection to be discovered. At lunchtime, when Ellie was fetching her sandwiches from the tack-room, Nigel Hunt appeared in the doorway and said, 'Where's that friend of yours – Amanda, is it? I told her to bed down my horse's stable while he was out, but she doesn't seem to have done it yet.'

Ellie looked back at him warily. 'Er...she's home,' she said.

'Gone home? Why? Was she ill?'

'No,' Ellie said. 'She was fed up.'

She wondered whether to explain at greater length, but Nigel merely shrugged as if the mood-swings of teenage girls were quite beyond him, and said, 'Does Frances know?'

'I don't think so.'

At that point Frances' head appeared round the doorway. She said crossly, 'Where's Amanda? Paula had to get all the ponies ready on her own. She only just made it in time for the lesson.' It wouldn't have occurred to Frances to help, of course; hairy ponies were beneath her notice.

'Apparently she's gone home,' Nigel Hunt said.

'What do you mean, gone home?' Frances demanded, looking at Ellie.

This really wasn't fair of Amanda, Ellie thought, leaving her to face both of them, as if it were her fault. 'She doesn't want to work here any more,' she told Frances.

Frances' neat features contracted into a frown. 'Well, she could have *said*. It's a bit much to clear off in the middle of the day without saying anything, when she had jobs to do.'

Nigel had lost interest. 'See my horse's bed gets

done, won't you?' he said to Frances, and sauntered off in the direction of the house, whistling.

'You'd better do that,' Frances told Ellie, 'and you can take Trojan out this afternoon instead of doing the tack. An hour's walking and steady trotting. You can go out in the woods. And when you come back you can help Paula with the four o'clock lesson.' She actually smiled, and Ellie realised that she'd be quite pretty if she didn't always look cross or superior. It occurred to her that Amanda's defection might mean that she was in favour herself, presenting a model of reliability by comparison. She wasn't sure whether this was a good thing or not, but at least she'd be getting an extra ride today. About to go, Frances turned back and said, 'Oh, and before you ride out, could you groom Florian and get him ready? Judith's coming at half past two.'

Ellie pulled a face. She didn't mind grooming Florian, not at all, but she wasn't sure that she wanted to act as Judith's unpaid girl groom. Whatever would Natalie and Amanda say about *that*, if they found out? However, after she'd bedded down the stable and eaten her sandwiches she tied Florian to a ring out in the yard and got to work, unable to help taking pride in doing a good job. It wasn't difficult to make such a handsome pony look smart, and she finished by brushing out his white mane and tail and oiling his hooves, so that he looked as if he were going to a show. Really, she couldn't understand why Judith didn't do all this sort of thing for herself. It was a bit much to own a pony and just turn up to ride it for a couple of hours.

When Judith arrived, she wasn't at all high-handed and in fact seemed embarrassed to find Ellie getting her pony ready for her. Flushing slightly, she said, 'I was going to do that. But thanks anyway. He looks lovely.'

Ellie stood back to admire her work. 'Are you going out for a nice long ride?' she asked enviously.

Judith didn't look in the least enthusiastic. 'I don't know how far I'll go. Are you riding this afternoon?'

'Only for an hour on Trojan, for slow exercise.'

'Can I come with you, then?' Judith said quickly. 'If you're going on your own?'

'Well, you can, but it won't be very interesting. I'm only allowed to walk and trot because Trojan's been lame, and I'll have to be back for half past three.'

'I don't mind,' Judith said promptly, to Ellie's surprise. 'I'd much rather go with you than on my own.'

Really, Judith was *peculiar*, Ellie thought as she led Trojan out into the yard and got ready to mount. Always drooping and moping about the place as if it was a punishment to spend her time here. Ellie couldn't make her out at all. Before they had ridden far along the muddy track through the woods, though, she began to understand. Judith, it was obvious, was not a confident rider, and with Florian she was definitely over-horsed. Her face taut, she sat tensely in the saddle as if expecting to be violently thrown off at any second. Her hands gripped the reins as if they were lifelines. The grey pony didn't like it. Judith's nervousness infected him and he snatched at the bit, jogging sideways and sometimes barging into placid Trojan, trying to get away from the pressure on his mouth. Ellie itched to interfere, to offer advice. She was sure Florian would have gone better for her; he didn't look like a difficult pony to ride. But Judith had only asked for company, not for a lesson. Ellie wished she'd come on her own after all. It wasn't often she had the chance to ride on her own and she liked to enjoy the peacefulness of the woods, but now her attention was solely taken up by the restless pair alongside. Ellie saw now why Judith had wanted the calming influence of Trojan, who was content to plod along quietly; but why had she bought a pony like Florian at all, since she clearly wasn't experienced enough to ride him properly? It was such a *waste*.

Before long, Judith acknowledged this by saying, 'It would be much better if we could swap ponies, really.'

'Don't you *like* Florian?' Ellie couldn't stop herself from asking.

'Oh, he's a beautiful pony, I know that,' Judith said. 'But he was my parents' choice, not mine.'

'You didn't *want* him?' Ellie burst out.

'I—' Judith's face twisted unhappily. She looked at Ellie, and evidently deciding that she could be trusted, said, 'My mum always wanted a pony when she was my age and I think she bought him more for herself than for me. He's not just a pony for riding about on, that's the trouble. My dad's business partner's got a son and daughter who go hunting and belong to the Pony Club, and they've got rosettes and silver cups all over their house. Mum and Dad think I can be like them, now I've got a pony too. They like the idea of going to these horsy events with a picnic hamper in the back of the car, drinking wine with this partner of Dad's and watching me win things. They want me to go to all the shows next year – they even want to buy a trailer – and with a pony like Florian they're going to expect me to do well. My mum and dad – they're the sort of people who *do* win things, if they set out to. But I'm not. And they expect me to be thrilled about it all, as if I'm the luckiest girl in the world. I know you think I am.'

Well, yes. But Judith certainly wouldn't win any prizes riding like that, Ellie thought. She tried not to feel envious, since Judith was so obviously worried, out of her depth. For herself, it would have been her wildest fantasy come true: a gorgeous pony, a trailer to take him to all the shows, and parents willing to fork out the enormous sums of money involved as well as providing a support team. All it needed to be completely idyllic would be Luke watching admiringly from the rails (in reality he wasn't remotely interested in horses, but there was no reason why the dream version shouldn't be) while she rode a stylish clear round against the clock. But for Judith it wasn't going to be idyllic. It would be humiliating, unless something could be done about her riding before Florian was spoiled. Judith's mum couldn't know much about horses, or she'd have realised that Florian wasn't the right pony to buy.

'I don't even like riding him,' Judith admitted. 'He won't walk or trot properly. He fusses about like this all the time. He doesn't like me, but when Paula rode him to show him to us, he looked fantastic. I know it's my fault but I don't know what to do about it.'

Ellie glanced across at her, dying to suggest that they swapped ponies, but knowing that it wasn't really a solution. 'Look, I'm no expert, but perhaps I could help a bit,' she said instead. 'If you sat right down in your saddle instead of perching forward, and tried to be more relaxed, then he'd relax too. And try not to hang on to the reins as if you think he's going to bolt off any second. He won't, not with Trojan here. Don't hold on to him so tightly.'

'All right,' Judith said doubtfully, shuffling in her saddle.

It worked, as Ellie knew it would. The grey pony stretched his neck and walked more calmly, and Judith began to look happier. She was even smiling by the time they got back to the yard.

'Thanks, Ellie,' she said. 'I'm really glad I went with you. Thanks for letting me come.'

She'd got Judith all wrong, Ellie realised as she led Trojan back to his box. Judith was really quite a nervous person: not snooty and superior as everyone at school thought, just pressured by her parents and scared out of her wits.

Lifts

At the beginning of October Luke passed his driving test at the second attempt. He had been having driving lessons whenever he could afford them and practising with his father in between. The immediate advantage was that he sometimes drove Amanda's mum's car to school, and occasionally gave the girls a lift. This, when it happened, gave Ellie abundant material for daydreams – even, if she were really lucky, for night-dreams as well. She always sat in the back, where she could admire the way the hair grew at the back of Luke's neck, and watch his reflection in the driver's mirror. She could see his dark eyelashes and the way his blue-grey eyes narrowed in concentration. Sometimes he caught her eye in the mirror and on one memorable occasion he smiled at her, a private smile that was shared between the two of them. His face tended to be serious, but when he smiled he looked entirely different: younger and mischievous. He had pointed eye-teeth, which added to his elfish look. He was thin-faced and always looked as if he needed a decent meal, which was odd, considering that he lived with Amanda's mum, who plied everyone with cakes, puddings, pies and biscuits as if she'd never heard of cholesterol. For Ellie, Luke's undernourished appearance was part of his charm; she couldn't have felt the same if he'd gone podgy and flabby under the strain of eating so much home cooking.

On the days when he had Art, his folder, a bulky affair with marbled binding tied together with tapes, rested on the parcel shelf behind Ellie's back seat. She would have loved to have a good look at what was in it, even scrappy sketches – anything that would give her an insight into his imagination. Sometimes, if he wasn't looking, she would turn round to see if there was a corner poking out with something psychologically revealing on it. She would have to wait until the sixth-form art exhibition in the summer to have a really good look. Once he left a book called *Stalin's Russia* on the back seat with a wad of notes tucked into it. His handwriting was bold and black with lots of swirling loops, the sort of handwriting she'd have expected to come from someone loud and extrovert.

Luke rarely said much to Ellie, apart from hello and goodbye; in fact he rarely said much at all, concentrating on his driving and leaving Natalie and Amanda to chatter. But Ellie didn't need him to take any notice of her; it was enough to be so close to him in the car that she could have reached out (if only she dared) to stroke his hair. The car was a two-door, so he had to tilt the seat forward for her to get out, and then stand holding the door. As she scrambled out inelegantly, clutching her bag, and paused to thank him for the lift, she was sometimes so close that she could smell the clean masculine smell of whatever shower-gel or deodorant he used. The lifts offered such marvellous opportunities for studying him at close range that her heart sank each time she saw Amanda standing by the conker tree, obviously intending to walk to school that day.

These rides in the car were spoiled only by the way Natalie behaved with Luke. She made no secret of liking him, though she wasn't single-mindedly devoted to him like Ellie; for her he was merely one of dozens of fanciable older boys. She always contrived to sit in the front, hitching up her short skirt and sitting sideways to turn round and talk to Amanda. Sometimes when Luke changed gear he couldn't avoid his hand brushing her leg. Ellie, watching hawk-eyed from the back seat, was sure this happened by design on Natalie's part, not by accident. When Luke apologised, Natalie simpered and looked at him in a way Ellie thought was frankly indecent. Fortunately, Ellie thought, Luke was probably safe from Natalie because of Rachel Ashton, who in Ellie's eyes was the most enviable girl in the world. (Now that Ellie knew more about Judith, she had stopped regarding her as joint leader in the good fortune stakes, leaving Rachel Ashton as clear winner.) According to Amanda, Rachel sometimes went up to Luke's bedroom when she came round, supposedly so that they could do their History homework together, although Amanda gave such lurid and no doubt exaggerated accounts of what really happened in there that Ellie felt herself going all hot and faint, imagining herself as Rachel. Rachel was a quiet and rather ordinary-looking girl, not a beauty like some in the sixth form, and was always friendly to Ellie when they both happened to be round at Amanda's – in fact, she spoke to Ellie more than Luke did, and was so pleasant that Ellie couldn't really resent her. But she couldn't have stood it if Luke had made any response to Natalie's come-ons. She consoled herself with the thought that Luke must think of Natalie as just a kid, even though Natalie was a little taller than Luke and could easily have been taken for the same age as him, especially out of uniform.

One afternoon, when they were all packed into the

car and Luke was about to pull out of the school drive, Natalie startled them all by shrieking: 'Stop! There's my sister!'

She pointed to the pedestrian barrier opposite the entrance to the drive. Standing there, or rather draped there, was an older version of Natalie. She had blonde hair that fell in strands over her eyes and a well-developed figure shown to advantage by a tight sweater and a long slit skirt. Her elbows were hooked back round the railings and one leg was crossed over the other, and her bold glance surveyed everyone who came down the drive. Some Year Eleven boys wolf-whistled and she smiled back, evidently pleased. She held a cigarette to her lips and blew smoke with a practised air.

'That's Lisa,' Natalie said to Luke as she un-fastened her seat-belt. 'She's staying with us. I forgot, we're going down town. See you tomorrow.'

She climbed out, slammed the door and darted across the road. The older girl disentangled herself from the railings to join Natalie and they turned together in the direction of the town centre. Amanda got into the front seat and belted herself in while Ellie watched them go, fascinated. Lisa took a packet and lighter out of her bag and passed a cigarette to Natalie, who lit up. Ellie saw that Luke was watching, too; then he released the handbrake and pulled out of the driveway, turning left in the opposite direction.

Ellie was shocked. 'Natalie's *smoking*!'

Amanda giggled. 'Well, people do.'

'Yes, but so close to school! Where any of the teachers could come out and see her!'

Luke's eyes met Ellie's briefly in the driver's mirror – although it could have been because he was about to slow down for a pedestrian crossing and was checking what was behind – and she wondered what he was thinking.

Amanda shrugged. 'She'd get a telling-off, that's all.'

'I didn't even know Natalie had a sister,' Ellie said.

'Yes, you did. Lisa's staying with them until she gets somewhere of her own – she's on the dole and now she's been kicked out of her flat. You obviously don't *listen*,' Amanda said scathingly. 'Natalie was talking about it the other day.'

Rebuffed, Ellie fell silent. Natalie was always dropping names into the conversation, usually those of her famous mates and other people Ellie had never heard of, so she had stopped taking close interest.

'I suppose they must have been twins,' Amanda said thoughtfully. 'Lisa looks about seventeen.'

Ellie remembered Natalie's dead brother. '*Oh*, you mean Lisa and...?' She stopped just in time, remembering that she wasn't supposed to mention the tragedy. Would it matter if Luke heard? He certainly wasn't the gossiping type.

'Liam.' Amanda frowned. 'I'm not sure if they were twins or not. He might have been a bit older. I don't think Natalie's ever said.'

Ellie said no more, because she thought it was rude to have a conversation that left Luke out when he was giving them a lift. Amanda and Natalie did it all the time: half-whispering, giggling, with references that Luke couldn't possibly have picked up even if he had wanted to, but Ellie thought it inconsiderate to ignore him and treat him as a chauffeur. She said no more, thinking that Natalie's family really did seem to have had more than its fair share of difficulties: the brother's death, the mother's alcohol problem, unemployment, and now an eviction. She wondered how Lisa was able to smile so cheerfully. She didn't look in the least worried by any of it, if her expression just now had been anything to go by; she had looked as if she were thinking of taking her pick of the sixth-form boys. *Tarty* was the word that came into Ellie's mind, although Mum hated the word and had told her not to use it: it was sexist, she said, and there was no male equivalent. But Lisa did look tarty, call it whatever you wanted.

Amanda yawned and stretched, and said, 'Three

lots of homework to do tonight. At least one of them's only History. It's not worth bothering for that stupid Wishart cretin.'

Luke said unexpectedly, 'Wishart? Does he teach your class? We have him for Modern European History. He's brilliant. The best History teacher I've ever had.'

'*Brilliant?*' Amanda pulled an incredulous face. 'You're kidding! He hasn't got a clue. You must have got him mixed up with someone else.'

'I haven't. He is brilliant,' Luke insisted. 'He knows so much, and he puts it across so well.'

'Yes, he does,' Ellie agreed, 'when the idiots and yobs let him.'

Amanda puffed out her breath slowly. 'Everyone knows he can't control a class. And who wants to listen to him rambling on, anyway?'

'You should try,' Luke suggested gently.

Amanda turned round to Ellie and rotated the tip of one forefinger against the side of her head. But Luke caught Ellie's eye in the mirror – there was no doubt about it this time – with an expression that said, *You know what I mean, don't you?* Yes, she did. Mr Wishart *would* be interesting, if he hadn't got off to such a bad start. The people in Luke's class wouldn't give him the wrong names or fight with rulers or make fun of the way he talked. They were serious students who read books like *Stalin's Russia*, and who would respect Mr Wishart for his knowledge and enthusiasm instead of writing him off as a nerd.

Ellie took great care with her History homework that night, warmed by the knowledge that Luke thought Mr Wishart worthy of respect. She felt that it was her duty, a way of saying *I know you're doing your best*. If he knew that even one person in the class was doing the work thoroughly and well, that might encourage him a bit. And of course it was more than one, because Samantha Warburton always got top grades, so did Greg, and there were at least three or four others, including Judith, who would work conscientiously for the most inept and least inspiring teacher.

Amanda went into town every Saturday afternoon now with Natalie, meeting Jonno and Darren and various other friends. Sometimes Ellie wondered why she was still friendly with Amanda. Amanda was changing, trying to be sophisticated and streetwise. She got her hair cut spikily and started wearing make-up every day; the school rules didn't allow obvious make-up, but both Amanda and Natalie got away with it. Ellie was always in such a rush in the morning that she wondered how they could fit in time to put on make-up, or what the point of it was, just for school. Mr Kershaw usually turned a blind eye, or perhaps he didn't even notice, but if any of the senior staff caught anyone in the lower school wearing too obvious make-up they took them to the Head of Year's office and made them scrub it all off. It didn't suit Amanda; whereas Natalie could easily be taken for seventeen or eighteen, Amanda looked as if she'd daubed her face with crayons.

'You ought to come with us one Saturday,' Amanda said to Ellie once or twice, 'unless you really *prefer* shovelling manure and being bossed about by Frances. You don't have to go every single week, do you?'

Ellie thought perhaps she might go, just once, to show Amanda that she wasn't intimidated. But not yet.

Next Friday evening, Amanda phoned Ellie at home. 'Do you want to come round tomorrow and stay the night? Mum and Bill are going to a party. Luke will be here—' she giggled mischievously '— some of the time, at least, but they said I could ask you to stay, for company.'

'Why didn't you ask Natalie?' Ellie said pointedly.

Amanda hesitated for long enough to make Ellie wonder whether she actually had asked Natalie first, but then she said, 'I'd rather you came.'

Back in favour, am I? Ellie thought.

'Mum and Bill don't really know Natalie. They suggested you,' Amanda explained.

Oh, so it was their idea, not yours. But while she was still wondering whether or not she wanted to go, Ellie found herself saying, 'OK then, I'll ask.'

Amanda's laughter rippled into her ear. 'Knew you wouldn't be able to resist.'

'I'll be at the stables till about five, though.'

'Yes, I know. I meant after that.'

Mum and Dad agreed straight away. Not so long ago, Ellie and Amanda had been in the habit of spending the night at each other's houses quite regularly. Whichever house they were at, they would share a bedroom and stay awake whispering and giggling far into the night, not settling down for sleep until a frustrated parent knocked on the door to demand peace and quiet. That seemed ages ago now: not just the visits but the sorts of things they had whispered and giggled about. Ellie wondered if it could possibly still be the same now.

She felt better as soon as she arrived. She had forgotten how Amanda dropped a year or two in age when she was with her parents, abandoning the sophisticated airs she put on for Natalie's benefit. At home, Amanda was a lot nicer; she stopped pretending.

'There's jacket potatoes in the oven, ready in about three-quarters of an hour, and sausages and soup to heat up. Lemon meringue pie in the fridge, and plenty of cakes and biscuits in the tin if you're still hungry.' Amanda's mum always seemed to imagine that people left in the house for more than an hour or two would wilt and die from starvation unless she provided abundantly for them. Self-conscious in her best clothes for the party, she looked as if they didn't really belong to her. She moved awkwardly in high heels and when she bent over the oven door to check the potatoes she tugged at the neck of her blouse as if she were afraid it was too low-cut. She smelled deliciously of perfume, but Ellie thought she looked a lot nicer, and less anxious, in the jeans and baggy jumpers she usually wore. Dressed like this, she was trying to be someone else. Sometimes grown-ups pretend, too, Ellie thought.

Amanda's mum gave them a lot of instructions to be sure to turn off the oven and to be careful with the gas fire, and to let Luke go to the front door if anyone rang. Bill, Amanda's stepfather, stood patiently meanwhile, jingling the car keys and not looking at all smart or dressed-up, in an ordinary jumper and cord trousers. Men didn't have to bother, a fact Ellie had often noticed in her own father. At last they were gone. Ellie's ears kept straining towards Luke's bedroom above the lounge – she was sure she had heard the floorboards creaking at one point – until she couldn't help asking, 'Did you say Luke was going to be in tonight?' It was Saturday, after all. Surely he and Rachel Ashton weren't going to spend the evening isolated in their respective rooms.

She spoke as casually as she could, but Amanda grinned and said, 'He's going out later, to pick Rachel up from the sports centre. She's playing in a squash match tonight. Then they're going round to some friend's house.'

'Doesn't Luke play?' Ellie asked, nurturing a secret hope that Luke would come down and eat with them, and at the same time feeling quite terrified in case he did, because she wouldn't know what to say to him.

'Sometimes. But this is a women's match.'

Luke did appear, but only briefly, after they had eaten and cleared up. He ate on his own in the kitchen and then came into the lounge, jingling a bunch of car keys in his hand. (Why did men always do that, Ellie wondered? There must be a male need to create an air of *Can't stand around talking – places to go, things to do.*)

'I'm off now,' he said. He was wearing black jeans and a black sweater with a split and unravelling shoulder seam, and his denim jacket was slung over one shoulder.

'Mum didn't say you were taking her car,' Amanda said. 'Does she know?'

'No, but I'm late and I'm giving someone a lift. She won't mind.'

'Giving who a lift?'

'Andy Crossland, as if it's any business of yours.'

Amanda's mouth fell open. 'What, Sandy Andy who got chucked out of the sixth form? Didn't know you still hung round with him.'

'I don't, but he lives just round the corner now and he's asked me for a lift, OK, Miss Spanish Inquisition? He's meeting someone after the squash match too, but his own car's packed up.'

'OK.' Amanda shrugged. 'Can we use your computer?'

'If you must. And only games. No messing about with my private files.'

Amanda made a moonstruck face. 'Love letters to Rachel?'

'History essays,' Luke said. 'Nothing you'd be interested in. See you later, then.'

'Don't get up to anything,' Amanda said archly. Luke pulled a face at her and closed the door.

'You've embarrassed him,' Ellie whispered to Amanda, who giggled and said, 'Only because you're here. He wouldn't care what I said otherwise.'

Ellie was astonished. 'What do you mean?'

Amanda shrugged, more interested in zapping from one TV channel to another with the hand-control.

This was a habit that drove Ellie's mum to an uncharacteristic pitch of annoyance if anyone did it at home, and Ellie was equally frustrated now, wanting to know exactly what Amanda was hinting at.

'Come on,' she insisted. 'What do you mean, only because I'm here?'

Amanda looked at her teasingly. 'He likes you.' She gave a long enough pause for Ellie to feel in danger of bursting with pleasure before adding, 'Only as a friend of his little stepsister, I mean. What did you think I meant?'

'Nothing,' Ellie mumbled.

'He said, I'd do better to go around with you than with Natalie. He said you're all right. I'll be less likely to get into trouble if I stick with you.'

'Oh, I see.' Ellie tried to work out whether this only meant Luke thought she was dull and sensible, safe. 'Giving you fatherly advice now, is he?'

Oops, foot in mouth. This was a tactless thing to say to Amanda, whose real father had gone to live in the States and only saw her once a year, but Amanda only said, 'Luke doesn't like Natalie. There, that's something else you've got in common, as well as both liking the Wishart creep.'

'Well. I'm getting used to Natalie now,' Ellie said, although she wasn't sure how true this was. Natalie could be easy and friendly one day, intolerable the next.

'Yeah? You still haven't been out with us on Saturday, have you? You said you were going to.'

'I will.' Ellie noticed that it was *us* now. *Us* meant not her. 'When? Next Saturday?'

'If you like,' Ellie said rashly. 'What do you do, anyway?'

'Oh, just hang about,' Amanda said. 'It's a laugh. So you'll definitely come then? What are you going to tell Frances?'

'I can have a Saturday off if I want to.' Ellie didn't like the suggestion that she wouldn't dare stand up to Frances. It would be easy. She could just say, 'Sorry, I can't come next week.' There might be all sorts of reasons: a family occasion, a wedding or something like that, for all Frances knew.

Amanda smiled. 'Good. You don't have to feel left out. You can come any time you want. Let's go upstairs now.'

She wanted to show Ellie her new fleece, and then they went into Luke's bedroom to play on the computer. Ellie hadn't been in there before and she couldn't help goggling, trying to take in everything she saw. The bed had a navy-blue duvet thrown carelessly over it and a pair of Luke's boots was under the desk, one of them knocked on its side with laces trailing. The lampshade was a dangly Indian thing made of purple fabric and bits of shells, and the bedside lamp was in the shape of a leaping fish. Luke had a small desk, a shelf above it loaded with history and art books, and a pegboard completely covered with art postcards and odd messages and leaflets, one or two addresses written in his bold handwriting. There was also an old black-and-white film poster and two large sketches, strange abstracts made up of inky swirls and spirals. Ellie gazed at it all adoringly. The room was pleasingly arty, fitting her idea of Luke.

'Did Luke draw those?' she asked Amanda, indicating the sketches.

Amanda looked up from plugging in the computer, smirking. 'Yes. Fascinated, aren't you? Want to find a souvenir to take away with you – a toenail clipping or a flake of dandruff?'

'Luke hasn't got dandruff,' Ellie said. She had studied the back of his head enough times to know. 'Who's this Sandy Andy person he's giving a lift to?'

'Oh, you know. You must have seen him. Great lanky bloke about a foot taller than Luke. Day-Glo orange hair.' Amanda put a disk in the CD drive and frowned at the screen, mouse-clicking on various icons. 'He was in Luke's year till he got thrown out for doing drugs. He lives in the next road.'

Ellie remembered hearing it talked about and could vaguely remember the orange hair, but she had only been in Year Eight at the time, and sixth-form doings had made little impact on her. 'You don't think *Luke* does drugs, do you?' she asked.

'How should I know? He'd hardly tell me if he did, would he? Come on then, let's play this game.' Amanda pulled over a stool for Ellie. 'This is how it goes—'

It was a quiz game, where you had to answer a question correctly to find your way round a maze of rooms in a haunted house. Amanda became childishly excited, holding her head while she racked her brains, shouting out the answers, fidgeting in her seat when she knew the answer and Ellie didn't. Ellie didn't mind that Amanda won both the first and the second rounds, she was so much like her old self. They could still have fun together.

After the game, Amanda wanted to watch a TV programme, and then they had cake and Coke and got ready for bed. They were lying awake talking when they heard Luke come home, and then a little later Amanda's mum and Bill returned from their party. Amanda's mum looked into the bedroom to see that the girls were safely in bed, and then Ellie dozed off in mid-conversation, waking later with the shock of not knowing where she was. She must have muttered an exclamation, because Amanda clicked the bedside light on and said, 'There's someone downstairs.'

Fear gripped Ellie's chest. She was fully awake, sitting up in her sleeping-bag, hugging herself with fright. 'A burglar?' What should they do first? Go downstairs, wake Amanda's parents, phone the police? She imagined weapons – knives, guns—

'No, not a burglar. Someone's come to the door. I can hear Mum and Bill talking to whoever it is.'

'Funny time of night for someone to come round!'

It wasn't an ordinary visitor, either: Ellie heard Bill's voice raised in dispute.

Amanda swung her legs out from under the duvet, feet thudding on the floor.

'Where are you—'

'Shh!' Amanda sidled past Ellie's camp-bed and crept to the window, pushing the curtain back. There was a pause, and then: 'There's a car outside. A police car.'

'But what—'

Amanda pulled on her dressing-gown. 'Wait here. I'm going down to see what's going on. I'll tell you as soon as I know.'

Left alone, Ellie shivered and huddled into the quilted bag. It wasn't cold but she felt sick and shaken. The police car must have brought bad news from home – something had happened to Mum or Dad or Becky, or all of them, while she wasn't there. Perhaps the house had burned down. Why didn't someone come and tell her? And then she heard heavy footsteps dashing up the stairs and past Amanda's door to Luke's room. Straining her ears, she heard Bill's voice, talking quickly, and then Luke answering, bleary and half-asleep at first, and then clearly enough for Ellie to hear through the wall: '*What?* But why?' Bill again, a long explanation, and then Luke, fiercely: 'Of course not! You don't seriously think I—'

More inaudible conversation, and then two pairs of feet went along the landing and downstairs. Amanda didn't come back to explain what was going on, but Ellie could hear more angry voices. Impatient, she crept out of bed and went out to the landing. It obviously wasn't a ghastly accident to her own family after all, but why did the police want Luke? Did he know something they wanted to find out? Something about drugs, perhaps? Would Luke be involved in drugs, like Andy with the orange hair? Or been copped for speeding? But Luke always drove so carefully—

She almost collided with Luke bounding back upstairs. Too late to dart back into Amanda's bedroom, she tried to get out of his way. He was wearing only a pair of jeans but was too preoccupied to mind Ellie seeing him half-dressed. With no sign of seeing her at all, he marched into his own room and slammed the door. Ellie stared after him, appalled by his expression. His face was taut, mouth closed bitterly, eyes dark with anger – or with fear, Ellie couldn't tell. She only knew that Luke looked like a stranger, and that something awful was happening.

Saturday Night

Amanda was crying when she came back to the bedroom, making no attempt to hide it. Ellie stared. Amanda grabbed a tissue from the box on a shelf and mopped at her eyes.

'Mum says you might as well come down too,' she sniffed. 'You must be wondering what on earth's going on.'

'What *is*?'

'The police – they've come to arrest Luke.'

'*Arrest*—'

'They're taking him away for questioning—'

'But why? What's he done?'

'Nothing!' Amanda snapped it out as if Ellie were the accuser. 'They're arresting him for theft. Suspicion of theft from an automobile, was what they said. And the way they said it – all formal, like he's a criminal, and they won't even let Bill go with him, not in the same car— We'd better go down, Mum said.'

Ellie pulled a sweatshirt over her pyjamas and followed Amanda. She couldn't understand what was happening, or why. It was like being hurled unexpectedly into a TV crime drama. Would they really want her down there? Would *Luke*?

Fully-dressed now, Luke was standing by the front door beside a uniformed policeman whose presence seemed to fill the entire entrance. A second policeman stood in the porch. Ellie's eyes went straight to Luke, but he was looking at no one, his face stony. *Surely* they couldn't drag him out into the middle of the night like this, no matter what he was supposed to have done?

Amanda went to her mum, who hugged her and looked over her head at Ellie. 'There must have been some mistake,' she said softly to the two girls. 'Luke will explain – if they let him. I don't know why he can't be questioned here,' she said, loudly enough for the policeman to hear.

'I've already explained that, Mrs Flynn,' the policeman said evenly. He had a tanned face and a neatly-trimmed beard and looked rather like the policeman who'd come to school to talk about their rights and responsibilities. What about Luke's right to sleep uninterrupted in his own bed?

Bill snatched up his car keys from the hall table. 'I'll be there,' he said to Luke, who showed no sign of hearing.

'Can't we all go?' Amanda cried.

'I don't think that's a good idea,' Amanda's mum said. 'We'll stay here and wait up. I'm sure it won't take long,' she added defiantly, aiming it at the policeman.

He made no response, and it was only when he took Luke's arm and steered him outside into the darkness that Ellie really believed Luke was being taken away.

'Luke!' Amanda cried out, as if she could stop him from going.

Luke looked round, once, his face still set in that hard unfamiliar look. It flashed through Ellie's mind that he looked like a prisoner in the dock, waiting for sentence. But what had he *done*?

Bill stepped back into the hall to give Amanda's mum a quick peck on the cheek. 'I'm putting in a complaint about this,' he told her quietly. 'It's outrageous.' And then he was gone, closing the door behind him.

Amanda's mum closed her eyes and stood still for a few moments, seeming deliberately to calm herself. Then she said to the girls, 'Come on. I'll make us some cocoa while we wait. I don't suppose they'll be more than an hour or so.'

'But Mum—' Amanda was crying again. 'What did that policeman *say*? How can he come round here and drag Luke away as if he's a criminal?'

'I don't know. I don't know what right he has to do that. Someone saw Luke arriving at the sports centre with that other boy, Andy Crossland, then waiting outside by himself. This person, whoever it was, assumed he was hanging around the parked cars. Apparently there have been a few break-ins lately, so the duty manager took the number of the car – of my car. And then later on someone reported a car break-in and a radio missing, so the manager phoned the police with the car number and they traced us through that. The first thing those policemen asked me was who'd been out in my car this evening. Of course I said no one, because the car was here in the drive when we got back. And then it turned out Luke had borrowed it—' She screwed up her face, frustrated with herself. 'If only I'd guessed, and said Luke had my permission, it might have made a difference – but once I'd let on that I didn't know he had the car, and that I'd no idea who Andy was, that seemed to be all they needed. This Andy's been in trouble with the police before, apparently, and it was a black mark against Luke just for being with him.'

'So what's happened to him – Andy, I mean?' Ellie asked, thinking that it must have been Andy who broke into the car. 'Is *he* at the police station? Has he been arrested too?'

'Luke wouldn't break into a car! Why should he?' Amanda demanded.

'I know. We all know that, but try telling that policeman. He's convinced that Luke did it. And not only this break-in, but all the others that have happened. No, Andy isn't being arrested,' she added, looking at Ellie. He didn't take the radio either – he couldn't have done, without Luke seeing him. He left the sports centre straight away with his girlfriend, apparently, and went to the pub down the road. The police have checked. But *why* they won't believe Luke – oh, it's so ridiculous—'

They all went through to the kitchen. Ellie was thinking of the exchange she had overheard through the bedroom walls, Luke bursting out with *Of course not! You don't seriously think I —* She was sure that Bill must have asked him whether he'd done it, and that was why Luke had looked so bitter, shutting himself off from everyone, rejecting their sympathy. His own father had had to ask him. Ellie felt that she could understand Luke's anger, and yet other people – the police – might take that cold, closed-off look as evidence of guilt, or anger at having been caught.

Ellie and Amanda sat down on stools while Amanda's mum took mugs and a jar of hot chocolate out of the cupboard. 'I suppose if *I'd* been waiting at the sports centre, it would have been all right,' she continued, banging the mugs down on the surface, 'but Luke's an eighteen-year-old boy, isn't he? And that makes him automatically a delinquent. Especially if he's seen *hanging around*. I wonder what the distinction is,' she said angrily, 'between *waiting* and *hanging around*? The person who reported him to the manager said he was hanging around the parked cars. Luke says yes, he did wait there for quite a long time – he did get out, he went to look for Rachel and then came back, and it was a clear night so he stood for a while looking at the stars.' Amanda's mum gave a hollow laugh. 'You can imagine how that went down, when he told them. Then after a while he went again to look for Rachel, and couldn't find her, so he left.'

Ellie listened, unable to say anything at all. She thought of Luke standing alone in the car park, looking up at the stars just as she did herself sometimes, and a stranger watching him, seeing only a malicious yob waiting to pick car locks. How can they *do* it, to Luke of all people, it's not *fair*, it's not *fair*, was what she wanted to say, but it sounded so childish. And the situation Luke had got into wasn't a childish one. Luke was over eighteen, an adult as far as the law was concerned. He couldn't even be accompanied by his father.

'But that's *awful!*' Amanda said. 'Didn't he tell them about waiting for Rachel?'

'Of course he did, but – unfortunately – there was a misunderstanding. Rachel got a lift with one of her other friends and so Luke missed her. The policeman seemed to find that suspicious – the fact that Rachel wasn't there to be picked up, to confirm what Luke said. Even though, when Luke realised she'd gone, he went round to this friend's house and met Rachel there.'

'We know he did! Otherwise he'd have been home earlier.' Amanda scrubbed at her face with the soggy tissue. 'What will they do to him now?'

Her mother was standing by the microwave, waiting for it to bleep. 'Question him again more thoroughly, I suppose, get a statement from him. If only it weren't the middle of the night... Bill's phoned the duty solicitor, and she'll go round to the police station. *Why* they can't simply accept what he says, or take a statement here instead of hauling him off there, I don't know. It's not as if he's ever been in trouble before, apart from the silly sorts of trouble most boys get themselves into at some time or another. He's done nothing to arouse suspicion – apart from taking the car without my knowledge, and being with someone who's known to the police. But neither of those things are *crimes*. Oh, I do wish he'd told me he wanted the car!'

'They'll have to bring him back soon,' Amanda said.

But they finished their cocoa and ran out of things to say to each other and still nothing happened. The cat jumped on to Ellie's lap and sat there purring, the only contented creature in the house, while the kitchen clock ticked slowly and its hands measured out the minutes with grudging slowness. Ellie's eyes ached in the bright kitchen light and Amanda's mum looked jaded, her eyelids smudged with the make-up she'd worn to the party. She didn't wear make-up very often and hadn't got it all off properly. At last she said, 'I think you two had better go to bed. There's no point all of us being exhausted tomorrow. I can't think why Bill hasn't phoned.'

Both girls protested, but Amanda's mum insisted and they had to give in.

Although Ellie was sure she wouldn't be able to sleep, she fell into a confusion of dreams and imaginings, seeing Luke in court, Luke handcuffed, Luke in a prison cell, Luke in a police mug-shot, full-face and profile.

She only woke up when Amanda nudged her and handed her a mug of tea.

'They're back,' she whispered. 'But it was about four o'clock in the morning before they let Luke go. And they put him in a *cell*.'

Ellie sat up blearily. She couldn't believe she'd slept at all, though she must have.

'But they let him out?'

'Yes, on bail. But it isn't all over yet. Bill and Mum are both furious. With the police, I mean.'

Ellie looked at her watch. Half-past nine. She hadn't slept so late for ages.

'Has Luke told you about it?'

'No, I haven't seen him. He's still asleep. Mum's getting breakfast if you want to come down.'

Breakfast was dismal and strained. Amanda's mum looked tired and defeated, lacking the energy to put on a brave face for the girls, even to be angry and disbelieving as she had been in the early hours of the morning. She told Ellie that Luke had been questioned extensively and at last released, but that he might still have to appear in court if charges were pressed. After breakfast she took a mug of tea up to Luke, and came down a while later looking as if she didn't quite know what to do.

'I'm sorry,' she said to Ellie. 'I was going to ask you to stay for lunch or all day if you wanted, but I'm afraid Luke's taking all this rather badly. Not that I blame him, but I think it might be easier if you went home. He's asked me to phone Rachel and find out whether the police have contacted her, but he doesn't even want to speak to her himself, not yet. Sorry,

Ellie! It's been a bit dismal for you, dragged into all this.'

'I don't mind,' Ellie said hastily. She did feel in the way, but she didn't want to go home without seeing Luke, without hearing his version of what had happened or seeing him restored to his usual self. However, none of that looked at all possible.

'You two could go and have lunch together at Burger King if you like. I'll give you the money,' Amanda's mum said hopefully, but Amanda shook her head and said, 'I don't want to go out.'

There was nothing for Ellie to do but go home. Amanda's mum drove her.

'You will come again when things are more normal, won't you?' she said outside Ellie's house.

'Yes,' Ellie said quickly. 'Ask Amanda to phone me! She will, won't she?'

'Oh yes, I'm sure she will,' Amanda's mum said, not looking at all sure.

They went indoors together. Amanda's mum explained briefly what had happened, refused offers of tea or coffee and left. And within five minutes, Ellie was having a furious row with her own parents.

'Oh, dear. What a difficult situation,' Mum said. She had made the tea anyway, and the three of them – Mum, Dad and Ellie – stood in the kitchen drinking it while Becky, at the table, crayoned a picture. 'I wonder if she's right to be so sure Luke didn't do it. I mean, surely the police must have grounds for suspicion.' Her expression plainly said, to Ellie, *I'm not sure we want you accepting lifts from Luke if he gets up to that sort of thing...*

Ellie exploded. 'How can you say that! When you've just been acting all sympathetic while Amanda's mum was here!' She plonked her mug down on the table, sloshing tea, and Becky tugged her drawing book out of the way with a squeal of alarm. 'You're just as bad as the police! He was there, so he must have done it – that's what you think!'

'Steady on, love,' Dad said. 'Mum wasn't saying that—'

'Yes, she was!'

Mum, surprised by the force of Ellie's outburst, retracted hastily. 'I know Luke wouldn't do something like that on his own. But he was with this other boy, who sounds a bit dubious by all accounts. Perhaps they did it together, as a dare or something. I was just wondering whether there's more to it than Amanda's family know about—'

'That's the same thing, isn't it? You think because he's been arrested he's already labelled a criminal!'

Becky's eyes were fixed on Ellie's face in concern. It was unusual for Ellie to shout.

'Calm down, Ellie, calm down,' Mum soothed. 'I

know you're upset, and it's not surprising after being up half the night, but—'

'That's not why I'm upset! I'm upset because it's so unfair and you're making it *worse!*'

There was a choking lump in Ellie's throat. She bolted out of the kitchen and up to her room, where she flung herself face down on the bed and gave way to a storm of tears.

On Monday, the story of Luke's arrest was all round the school. By unspoken agreement, neither Ellie nor Amanda mentioned what had happened when they met Natalie at the street corner. It didn't occur to Ellie that anyone else would know, but hardly were they inside the school gates when Jamie Day bounded up and said gleefully to Amanda, 'Is it true your brother's been nicked?'

'You what?' Natalie exclaimed before Amanda could answer.

By lunchtime, Amanda wanted to hide from everyone. There was no hope of keeping Luke's arrest secret; Jamie's brother's friend had been at the sports centre on Saturday evening, and the man who'd reported the missing radio was someone who refereed seven-a-side football for the league Jamie's brother played in on Sundays. Besides, Rachel's friend, the one who'd given her a lift, had told people in the sixth form, and so the story had spread, variously embellished: Luke and Andy were in prison...Luke and Andy had been arrested for drug-dealing...Luke was going to be expelled...

Ellie was relieved when Jo and Lynette asked her to come out for netball practice at lunchtime. Neither of them mentioned the arrest, and it was a relief to stop thinking about it. Just for half an hour, she could concentrate on footwork and passing, and wonder how it was that Jo, the smallest of the players, could successfully get the ball from much taller people. Amanda, who hated sport, came anyway and sat at the side of the court to watch. But the subject couldn't be forgotten for long.

'It's not just that everyone *knows*,' Amanda told Ellie in the library at lunchtime. 'It's the way they're all so excited about it! It's like it was some TV soap. And even worse is that so many people assume he *did* it.'

Ellie had heard them. Jamie, Jason, Matthew: 'Tough luck, getting nicked.' 'He should have been more careful.' 'Bit daft doing that car in full view of the entrance.' Damien: 'Got any stereos going cheap then, 'Manda?' And even Natalie: 'I shouldn't worry. I expect he'll get away with it.' So many people had a comment to make, an opinion to offer.

Amanda had become an unwilling celebrity. And if it was like this for her, Ellie thought, what must Luke be going through? Someone brasher might have laughed it off, enjoyed the attention, but Luke wouldn't want that sort of notoriety. He had driven to school by himself this morning, not offering to bring the girls, and by afternoon registration Ellie noticed that the car was gone from its parking place. She guessed that Luke had gone home as soon as his lessons for the day were finished, not wanting to hang around in the sixth-form common-room. She didn't blame him.

'If he didn't do it, then why's he skulking about like a criminal?' Jason said on the way to Maths, their last lesson. 'Looks guilty to me.'

Ellie thought Amanda was going to hit him. She would have liked to hit him herself, for his malicious enjoyment of the day's gossip.

'Sod off, Jason,' Amanda hissed. 'What do you know? Been watching too much *Crimewatch*?'

Ellie thought perhaps she and Amanda ought to walk around with a banner saying LUKE FLYNN IS INNOCENT OK. How did that saying go – *a man is innocent until he's proved guilty?* It didn't seem to be working. It seemed more like *You're guilty until you're proved innocent*.

Concentrating on Maths was quite impossible.

'What will happen if Luke goes to court?' Amanda asked Ellie under cover of their equations worksheets.

'What will happen if they decide he's guilty?'

Ellie didn't know. She could think of nothing that would make Amanda feel better, apart from refusing to believe that Luke had done anything wrong.

Hanging Around

On Thursday lunchtime in the library, Ellie saw Greg Batt bent in concentration over a table. The book she was returning was the First World War one he'd recommended; she went over to tell him about it.

'Thanks for this,' she said, showing him. 'It was really good, like you said.'

Greg glanced round quickly, then bent over his book again. 'Glad you liked it,' he mumbled. Ellie looked at what he was doing. He had out a book of letters, decorative alphabets, all loops and swooping lines bending back on themselves and knotting through each other. Looking more closely, she saw that some of the lines, after twining around in several directions, finished up as the surprised faces of serpents or dragons, with flickering tongues and bulgy eyes. Greg was copying some of them on to a piece of card. When he saw her looking, he quickly covered the card with his hand, but then moved it slowly aside so that she could read what the letters said. His own name, Greg Batt, in fine black pen, embellished with snakes and curlicues.

'That's lovely!' Ellie said.

'Do you like it?' Greg looked at her, a quick glance from his magnified eyes, and then he turned back to his desk as if he couldn't stand looking at her for more than a second at a time. Then he showed her the cover of the book he was copying from, *Celtic Art*. 'For the lettering project we're doing in Art,' he explained.

'Da da da da da da da da da, *Batman!*' The chanting voice from behind made them both jump. Ellie turned to see Damien's grinning face. 'It's the Caped Crusader,' he boomed in a deep American accent, 'discovered on an mystery assignation with Ellie Fant, secret agent. Stay tooned, fans, for the next thrilling instalment from Gotham City.'

Greg closed his eyes wearily. 'I don't think I've ever seen you in the library before,' he said to Damien. 'They don't have many comic books, if that's what you're after.'

'Yes they do,' Damien said, triumphantly holding out the book he'd chosen, *Asterix the Gaul*.

'Do you want that book issued?' Mrs Abbot called from the desk. It was her way of reminding Damien that he was in the library and not supposed to be having conversations at the top of his voice.

'Yeah, all right. Reado! Come on!' he shouted to Jason Read, who was leafing through a computer magazine. Mrs Abbot rolled her eyes and sighed.

'Imaginative nickname, isn't it, for someone called Read?' Greg said witheringly to Ellie.

That evening Mum asked Ellie if she'd like to go with her to collect Becky from a friend's birthday party. Ellie wasn't sure why she agreed – things were still strained between Mum and herself, after their argument – but she'd just finished three lots of homework and thought she might treat herself to a magazine on the way back. Mum had to buy emergency supplies of washing powder, so they stopped off at a general store. While Mum chose what she wanted, Ellie looked at the rows of magazines, flicking through *Horse and Pony* and *Mizz* and trying to stop Becky from pulling the newspapers about.

'Hello, Ellie,' said a voice behind her.

She turned to see Mr Wishart standing there. He was wearing jeans and a denim shirt and held a bottle of wine wrapped in tissue paper.

Ellie swallowed. 'Oh, hello.' It was always a shock when you saw teachers out of school. It was easy to forget that they had lives of their own.

Mum turned round with her change, looking

interested. Ellie wondered whether she ought to introduce Mr Wishart – she wasn't very good at that sort of thing, and besides Mum was wearing her baggy checked trousers that Ellie thought made her look like a circus clown. But Mr Wishart transferred the bottle to his left hand, held out his right to Mum and said, 'Hello – Mrs Byrne? I'm Jeremy Wishart and I teach Elena's class for History.' There wasn't a hint of his classroom nervousness.

Mum smiled back and said, 'Pleased to meet you. I suppose you bump into pupils all the time if you live so close to the school.'

'Oh, I don't live here,' Mr Wishart said. 'I've been invited for a meal with friends.' He held out the bottle of wine and then looked at his watch. 'Mustn't be late. See you tomorrow, Ellie.'

'What a nice young man,' Mum said, looking out of the door after him as he left. 'Good-looking, too. I bet he's popular with the girls.'

Oh, Mum! You don't know anything, Ellie thought. But Mum's impression was understandable: Mr Wishart had seemed like any other nice-looking young man – casual, pleasant, not an outcast but someone who had friends and got invited out. Perhaps that was his real self, the self he'd prefer to be, and the classroom version was one foisted on him by Year Nine.

*

Next day there was more trouble. Someone had written I HATE WISHART and WISHART IS A MORON on one of the tables in the History classroom. Mr Wishart kept Eduardo behind to account for it. At the end of break, Eduardo arrived grinning outside the Science lab, where the rest of the form were gathering.

'Hardly likely to write it on my own desk, am I?' he told his friends. 'Even Wishart had to admit I'm not enough of a berk for that. And I showed him it wasn't even my writing. 'Course, he didn't say sorry or anything.'

'How does he know it was our class, anyway?' Matthew wondered.

'Said he knew it appeared there between two and three o'clock on Wednesday, because one of his sixth form showed it to him first thing next morning and said it hadn't been there period four.'

'Nice of them,' Damien said. 'How did it go – *"Oh I say, Mr Wishart, sir, do come and have a look at this. Whatever can it mean, sir?"'*

'So anyway,' Eduardo continued, 'he's convinced it was one of us.'

'Do you suppose he'll keep the evidence,' Sanjay said, 'for handwriting analysis? But then everyone who sits at that desk would read it—'

'I bet it was a joint effort,' Natalie said. 'People from all his different classes adding their bit. Everyone hates Wishart.'

'Oh, do lay off,' Greg said in his detached way, not looking at anyone. 'Mr Wishart's all right if you give him a chance.'

Damien hooted. 'Fan of his, are you, Batty? Well, that makes sense. Two weirdos together.'

Really, if it weren't for Natalie and her grudge, Mr Wishart wouldn't be doing so badly by now; the boys would have bored themselves with their baiting and started picking on someone else. But with Natalie there, the class resembled an explosive charge with the minutes ticking away on the timing device. Natalie's behaviour in her other lessons wasn't too bad – not particularly good, either, but she'd managed to stay out of major trouble. Ellie hoped that eventually she'd stop disrupting the History lessons too.

Natalie's latest gambit was to shout out at Mr Wishart in the corridors or quad. She had once heard Mrs Dar address him as Jeremy, and for some reason she considered this a huge joke. Whenever she saw him out of the classroom she would shout out, 'I say, Jeremy,' to make him turn round. She had a way of braying it, 'Jewwem-eah,' that made it sound upper-class and affected. If Mr Wishart ever challenged her (which he soon learned not to do) she would say innocently, 'I was just calling out to Jeremy Holtby, that boy over there,' and get away with it.

By now, Mr Wishart gave the impression that he was dashing from place to place with imaginary ear-muffs clamped to his head. Ellie felt sure that Natalie must haunt the poor man in nightmares, even when he wasn't at school. She suspected that it was Natalie who had written on the desk, but didn't say so. Some things were better left to die down quietly.

'Coming out for netball practice?' Lynette asked Ellie, at the end of Science.

'Yes, OK,' Ellie said. 'Coming, Amanda?'

'No, got to finish my Geography homework for this afternoon,' Amanda said. 'See you later.'

Ellie left the form-room with Jo and Lynette, heading for the PE changing rooms near the main entrance. A slim girl dressed in black was hurrying along the path from the sixth-form centre, towards the point where the two paths crossed. She walked with her head bent, a hand to her mouth, her brown hair flopping over her face. It was Rachel Ashton. Ellie hadn't seen her since Luke's arrest, and wondered what to say. But Rachel glanced up, recognised her, made a dismissive gesture with her hand and turned her face away. Ellie saw that she was crying, really crying, her whole body shaking with suppressed sobs. Before she reached them she left the path and broke into a run, holding an arm across her eyes. She ran blindly, stumbling on the grass, as if all she wanted was to find somewhere to hide.

'Isn't that Luke's girlfriend?' Jo said.

'Yes.' Ellie turned to watch Rachel as she disappeared in the direction of a clump of trees on the far side of the playing field. She thought something awful must have happened, such as Luke being dragged off again in a police car, but at that moment she saw Luke himself, walking from the sixth-form centre with another boy. For a moment she expected him to run after Rachel, but he was clearly not hurrying and didn't seem to have seen her. The other boy was talking non-stop and Luke was listening, head down, occasionally nodding and looking very serious.

'What's all that about, then?' Lynette asked.

Ellie shook her head.

Jo said, 'That's the trouble with Lurve. I don't know why anyone bothers with it. It turns normal people into drooping soggy heaps.'

'Sympathetic, or what?' Lynette mocked. She broke into a run, flicking a hand at Jo's head as she passed.

Ellie had to wait till registration to consult Amanda, who said matter-of-factly, 'Oh, I know. Luke's dumped her.'

'But *why?*'

'How would I know? He's hardly going to have cosy chats with me about his love-life, is he?' Amanda picked at a brtoken fingernail. 'All I know is he's walking round like a zombie and she's weeping buckets. He Wants To Be Alone, that's what Mum says, like Marlene Whatsit in some ancient film.'

Dumped. Ellie didn't like the word, even though everyone used it; it made people sound like bits of rubbish, carted off to the tip. She couldn't imagine Luke doing the dumping. And why *now*, when you'd have thought he'd want Rachel's support?

'You must have some idea,' she persisted.

'I haven't! P'raps he thinks she let him down at the weekend. P'raps he thinks it's her fault, going off to her friend's and leaving him standing around.' Amanda flipped open her homework diary. 'P'raps she thinks he *did* it.'

'Oh, but she wouldn't !'

Amanda shrugged. 'Look at all this homework,' she grumped. 'Just got the Geography done, but there's still three-and-a-bit lots to do, *and* a Science test on Monday. Thank God it's Friday.' She looked up at Ellie. 'You're still coming down town with me and Natalie tomorrow, aren't you?'

'Oh – yes, if you're going.' Absorbed in Luke's predicament, Ellie had almost forgotten about it, and wasn't sure she wanted to go anyway. But she couldn't back out now – Amanda was expecting her to go.

By Saturday mid-morning, Ellie still hadn't told Frances she was going home at lunchtime. Frances collared her near the tack-room after the ride, and started on a list of instructions. 'Nigel wants Spanish Ledge given a thorough grooming. Then after lunch, once you've got the ponies ready for the two o'clock lesson, you can empty out all those new sacks of feed that have just arrived. Then there's—'

Ellie shuffled her feet on the gravel. 'Actually I can't stay this afternoon. I've got to go somewhere else.'

'Oh?' Frances didn't look at all pleased. 'Well, it would have been helpful if you'd told me before. I assumed you'd be here.'

Yes, you do, don't you? Ellie felt like saying, Natalie-style, but instead she said, 'It's only for this week. I'll be here as usual next Saturday. I'll pay full price for my lesson if you want.'

'That's up to you. You'll have time to do the lunchtime watering before you go, won't you?'

Ellie went off to start with the livery yard. As she passed Florian's stable, Judith came out without seeing her, went round to the main yard and then came back again, looking agitated. Thinking there might be something wrong with Florian, Ellie put down the two buckets she was carrying and followed Judith into the livery tack-room. Judith was ferreting about in a bag.

'What's wrong?' Ellie said.

Judith sniffed and looked up at Ellie with red-rimmed eyes. 'My mum and dad will kill me, that's all.'

'Why? What have you done?'

'Lost my new headcollar. I can't find it anywhere,' Judith sniffed, continuing to look about in a hopeless way.

'It's bound to be here somewhere. What's it like?'

'Blue webbing, brand new.'

'Someone else has picked it up by mistake, that's all. It'll turn up,' Ellie said. Really, Judith was making an unnecessary fuss. Things were always going missing and turning up again, left in stables, buried in hay or put on the wrong peg.

'But it's got a disc clipped to it with Florian's name on one side and mine on the other,' Judith said. 'No one could take it by mistake. It was hanging here on my peg.'

'They might not have noticed. Honestly, it'll be all right, I bet.'

'I don't dare tell Mum and Dad.' Judith's face was stiff and frightened. 'They're bound to think it's my fault for not looking after my things properly. When they've spent all this money getting me everything I need.'

'Don't tell them, then.' Ellie tried not to sound impatient. 'You don't know yet that it's definitely lost. Have another look round later when all the other livery people have put their stuff back in here.'

'Someone's taken it,' Judith insisted. 'On purpose. Stolen it.'

'Don't be daft,' Ellie said. 'That sort of thing doesn't happen here.'

But she hadn't known until a week ago that things got nicked from the sports centre car park, either. What Judith had said niggled at her all the way home. Was someone going to get hauled in to face police questioning for nicking Judith's headcollar? Would the police be bothered about something so insignificant? But she couldn't really believe that anyone was stealing things from the stables. On Monday she would ask Judith whether the headcollar had turned up; she was prepared to bet it would have done. Ellie didn't like the threat of nasty things happening wherever she went.

She caught the lunchtime bus home, in time to shower and change and get another bus to the town centre.

'Where are you off to, then?' Mum said when Ellie

came downstairs in her new jeans and jumper and made herself a sandwich for a quick lunch.

'Out with Amanda,' Ellie said. She didn't feel like giving a fuller explanation.

'What time will you be back?'

'Don't know,' Ellie said. She didn't usually speak to Mum in that bored, sulky way and she was surprised how easily it came to her. It didn't make her feel good, though. Her uneasy mood increased as the bus neared the town centre. She began to feel apprehensive, almost wishing it were time to go home and the bus was heading in the opposite direction. It would have been nicer to spend the afternoon with Amanda, just the two of them. The incident with Luke had brought back their old closeness and it would have been fun to go shopping or swimming together instead of bothering with Natalie and her friends.

Hagley Heath had an old part, with a market cross and a big town hall and some old-fashioned shops, but the main shopping area was a modern pedestrianised precinct. Ellie had arranged to meet Amanda outside W. H. Smith's. She thought Amanda would be on her own and that they'd go somewhere else to meet the others, but instead there was a whole group of them, sitting on the concrete edge of the flower beds. A boy lobbed a screwed-up chip paper at a pigeon. Amanda was there, in a short tight skirt that didn't suit her. Natalie, in a leather jacket with all black underneath. And four others, looking at Ellie with bored interest: three boys and a girl. She recognised Jonno, and the boy called Darren from Year Eleven at school, but didn't know the other two. The girl took a cigarette out of her mouth to smile lazily but none of them said anything.

'Hi, Ellie,' Amanda said. 'You managed to escape then.'

'Hi,' Natalie said, getting to her feet. 'Where shall we go first?'

The boys looked at Ellie as if they were thinking *Is she with us? Who is she, somebody's kid sister?* No one told her the names of the two she didn't know, and she didn't like to ask. She had thought Jonno was Natalie's boyfriend, but it was the other boy, the taller one, who had his arm round Natalie's shoulders.

'HMV,' Jonno said.

The HMV shop was at the other end of the precinct. They began to walk slowly through the Saturday crowds. One of the boys said something that made the girl laugh in a loud cackly way. Ellie reddened, feeling sure the remark had been about her.

'Who are they?' she whispered to Amanda. 'What are their names?'

'Jonno and Darren – well, you know them. Sophie, and Lee,' Amanda said. 'Natalie's going out with him now.'

Lee was tall and skinny, with an aggressively short haircut. He and Natalie walked with their arms round each other's waists. Jonno, thickset with hair slicked back with gel, linked arms with Sophie. The smaller boy called Darren, who had dark hair and a sharp foxy face, walked next to Amanda, occasionally kicking at an empty can or jumping up to balance on the edge of a concrete flower bed. They were the sort of boys Ellie would cross the road to avoid if she were on her own. Walking abreast, the whole group took up a lot of the available space; a woman with a pushchair tutted and steered round them.

Sophie detached herself from Jonno to speak to Ellie. 'You're the one who hangs around at the stables, right?' She had dark hair cut very short at the back and in a long fringe at the front, over eyes ringed with black make-up.

'I help out on Saturdays,' Ellie said. 'Usually.'

'I used to go up there,' Sophie said, 'till I grew out of it, when I was about – eight. Got sick of those bossy instructresses, like little Hitlers with their whips and boots.' She laughed. 'I bet you've got My Little Pony at home, right?'

'No,' Ellie said. 'I grew out of it when I was about five.'

She couldn't usually think of sharp replies and felt rather pleased with herself. Sophie laughed again. She had a way of making a laugh sound like a threat. She went back to Jonno and led the way inside the HMV shop. They spent a long time in there, while Sophie and Jonno kept asking for CDs to be played and then changing their minds. Ellie wandered off and looked at videos, not wanting to discuss her preferences with the others. Amanda was giggling rather a lot, looking at the racks with Darren. At last Jonno chose two CDs and then they went into two fashion shops, where Natalie and Sophie pulled various clothes off the rails and stuffed them back anyhow.

'Now where?' Natalie said when they came out without buying anything.

Sophie looked up and down the street. Her expression was disdainful, as if she'd already been everywhere and done everything.

'What time's the film start?'

'Half four.'

'Let's wait in the park then,' Sophie decided. 'I'm fed up with the shops.'

Amanda hadn't mentioned going to see a film, though it seemed to be agreed. Mentally, Ellie went through the contents of her purse, deciding she could just about manage it. She hoped it was something she wanted to see. If Amanda weren't here she'd have gone home by now.

On the way to the park, there was a diversion into Tesco's. Sophie said she needed more cigarettes and the others wanted lager. Jonno, the nearest in age to eighteen, was dispatched to the checkout and the cigarettes counter while the others bought crisps and chocolate. Darren got hold of an empty trolley, leaned across it with legs flung out and went skittering down one of the aisles, making a young mother snatch her wandering infant out of his path.

'He's daft,' Amanda said fondly.

Ellie thought he was an idiot. 'Can you lend me a pound?' she whispered to Amanda. She wasn't going to have enough for the cinema *and* crisps.

'Here.' Amanda took out her purse and handed over a pound coin. She was wearing too much eye make-up; it had gone smudgy and smeary round her eyes.

In the park, they all piled on to a bench near the duck pond. It was a cold grey day, the wind ruffling the surface and making browned leaves rain down from the trees in gusts. Jonno started telling them a complicated story about getting the better of someone at the garage where he worked. Sophie unwrapped her cigarettes, lit one for herself and then passed the packet round. To Ellie's surprise, Amanda took one and then handed the pack to her. Ellie shook her head.

'Don't you smoke then – what's your name – Ellie?' Sophie asked condescendingly. 'No, I suppose not. You're a good little Pony Club girl, aren't you? Mummy and Daddy wouldn't like it.'

Natalie laughed. 'I bet you've never even tried, have you, Ell?'

Ellie hadn't, and didn't want to, but suddenly she was the centre of interest. She didn't like the way they were all looking at her as if she were peculiar, retarded. She felt hot and uncomfortable and about eight years old.

'Go on,' Amanda said, thrusting the packet towards her. 'I didn't like it at first.'

Ellie knew that Amanda's parents would be furious if they found out she smoked. Hers would be, too, but hardly meaning to she reached out and took a cigarette. Now she had to actually smoke the thing. She tried to hold it nonchalantly, the way she'd seen other people do it. Sophie held out the lighter for her and Ellie put the cigarette between her lips and held it there. The flame spurted up in front of her face.

'You have to breathe in, stupid,' Sophie said, laughing.

Lee muttered something to Natalie, who threw

back her head and laughed, a scornful cackle.

'Who's your friend?' Darren said to Amanda. 'Is she allowed to be out without Mummy?'

Amanda looked sidelong at Ellie, but said nothing. Ellie tried breathing in. A great gulp of hot smoke went into her lungs and seared her eyes. She wanted to choke, but she wasn't going to in front of the others. What was it doing to her, inside? She remembered lessons on smokers' cancer and imagined her lungs rotting and melting away at the very first whiff. It was awful. Why did people like it? She left it as long as she could before putting the cigarette to her lips again. Perhaps she needn't breathe in this time; she could just pretend. How long would it take for a cigarette to burn down, by itself?

Sophie nudged Jonno. 'God, I was on ten a day by the time I was her age.'

Fortunately, the others had found another source of interest and stopped watching her.

'Look at this,' Lee said, nudging Natalie.

A man on his own, a man of about sixty with a dachshund dog, was coming slowly towards them round the side of the pond. He was dressed in a bow tie and smart anorak and leather slippers, and Ellie thought he was probably someone's grandfather.

'Wotcha, Grandad,' Lee shouted out.

'Ooh, that's some hound,' Sophie called. 'I bet he's

fierce. Had they run out of Rottweilers?'

'Rrruff, rrruff,' Darren yapped.

Amanda giggled, and Natalie called out, 'Look, he can't afford a proper pair of shoes. Shall we have a whip-round? They've got some in the Help the Aged shop.'

'Great bow tie,' Jonno added. 'My old teddy bear used to have one just like that.'

They all shrieked with laughter at each other's jokes. The man didn't respond. He looked at them once and then quickened his pace, pulling the dachshund after him. Darren lobbed an empty can after them, making the dog look round and then scamper against its owner's legs.

They're just yobs, Ellie thought. She felt sorry for the old man, who hadn't even dared to answer back. People ought to be able to walk their dogs in the park without being jeered at. She remembered Mr Wishart telling them in History that some people were so fiercely anti-German in the First World War that they stoned dachshund dogs to death in the street. She had found it hard to believe that ordinary people could do something so cruel and pointless, but it wasn't so very different from the way Jonno and the others were treating the old man. Picking on him, just because he was outnumbered. What would Mum and Dad say if they could see her? Supposing one of the neighbours came through the park now, or even her parents with Becky? She felt ashamed, especially when they got up from the bench to go to the cinema, leaving a strewn mess of fag ends and beer cans. Ellie took the chance to stub out her cigarette. There was a litter bin a few yards away but she didn't dare to pick up any of the rubbish, thinking of the *good little girl* tag. She put her own crisp packet in her pocket to throw away later, wrapping the cigarette end in it.

It was even worse when they arrived at the cinema. She should have guessed that the film, *Deadly Double*, was classified fifteen and over.

'Don't worry, you'll get in, no problem,' Amanda said, seeing her dithering as she looked at the posters outside. She was right. Ellie hid herself at the back of the group and a bored attendant issued the tickets without even glancing at her.

Natalie led the way upstairs and they all bundled into a back row. Ellie sat at one end, with Amanda next to her and Darren on Amanda's other side. The others seemed more interested in chatting and laughing and passing a rustly bag of sweets along the row than in watching the film, not stopping even when a man in front turned round to hiss, 'Shut up, can't you! Some of us are trying to watch the film!'

It was a thriller, very fast-paced and noisy, with car chases, shoot-outs and writhing bodies. It wasn't the sort of film Ellie would have chosen but she was fascinated in spite of herself. She turned to Amanda to say something and realised that Amanda and Darren weren't watching the film at all. They were kissing. From then on Ellie could hardly keep her attention on the screen at all, alert to every movement on her right. Amanda! Behaving like that, with a nerd like Darren! Ellie's resentment towards Amanda sharpened: Amanda had let her down badly this afternoon. Ellie had never known her to behave in this mindless way before – giggling at anything, going along with the others no matter what they did. But then, Ellie thought, isn't that what I'm doing, too?

When they came out of the cinema into the lit-up evening street, Natalie said she was hungry and Lee suggested going to McDonald's.

'I'm going home,' Ellie told Amanda, who was still wrapped round Darren.

'It's past her bedtime,' Sophie giggled.

'Oh, do you have to?' Amanda complained.

Yes, Ellie did. It was nearly seven o'clock and her parents didn't know where she was. Besides, she'd had enough. She walked by herself to the bus station, where she had a long wait.

'You're late back,' Mum said when she got in, though not crossly – she was still trying to make amends. 'Had a good time?'

Ellie shrugged, her new bolshie teenager manner returning all by itself. She wondered whether Mum could smell cigarette smoke. 'It was all right,' she said, although she had hated it. All of it.

Luke

Ellie was getting ready for bed when Amanda telephoned.

'What do you want?' Ellie huffed.

A pause, and then: 'Listen, I'm sorry about today. Really sorry. I know you had an awful time. Those two, Sophie and Lee, I've not seen them before and they're not very nice, are they?'

'I'm surprised you noticed,' Ellie said. 'You were so busy throwing yourself at Darren and snogging in the cinema.'

An embarrassed laugh. 'I know. I can't believe I did that. I'm not going out with Darren or anything and I don't even like him that much, any more.'

'Looked like it,' Ellie said acidly. 'It was gross. I really enjoyed being elbowed out into the aisle by you two, let me tell you.'

'OK, I said I'm sorry. I'll say it again. *I'm sorry. I'm really, really sorry*. Will that do? Or would you like me to write you a letter? Have it announced on the six o'clock news?'

'All right then, you're sorry,' Ellie relented. 'So am I. Sorry I bothered to come. Sorry I gave up an afternoon at the stables just for that. And about the – the you-know-what,' she added, meaning the smoking. Mum and Dad probably couldn't hear through the wall, but you could never be sure. 'I must have been mad to try it. So must you.'

'OK. I, Amanda Flynn, solemnly admit to being certified mad. Never again will I disgrace myself in a public park or cinema and offend my best friend Ellie. I'll write it down and sign it in blood if you want. And now can I tell you the other reason I've phoned? Mum said I could invite you round for lunch tomorrow. To make up for last week when she packed you off home. Luke won't be here so you'll have to put up with me. You will come, won't you?'

Amanda's mum was in the kitchen when Ellie arrived, piling things in the sink. The room was full of wonderful warm smells, the back door open to the garden. 'Amanda's gone to Tesco's with Bill, to get a few bits and pieces,' she said. 'Let me get you a drink. I'm just about to tidy myself up.' She poured Ellie a glass of lemonade and put ice and a chunk of lemon in it. 'They won't be long.'

She went upstairs, and Ellie took her drink out into the garden. It was a warm day, as if the season had turned itself round and gone back into late summer. A few late bees had gathered on the ice-plant and there were blackberries ripening in the untidy hedge. Ellie loved the wildness of Amanda's garden. From habit, she wandered down past the currant bushes towards the swing tree and then stopped in confusion. Luke was sitting on the swing with his back to her, humming, pushing himself gently backwards and forwards. He was wearing black jeans and his black sweater with the shoulder seam that was coming unravelled and a white T-shirt underneath – the same clothes he had worn on the night of the arrest. She was so close that she could see the tanned back of his neck and the way his hair grew thickly down to a point, so familiar to her from the car journeys. The black-and-white cat sprawled near him on the grass, sunning itself.

Her first instinct was to turn and go back up to the house. She felt nervous of Luke, not having spoken to him since the night of the arrest, and never before on her own. But then what if he turned round and saw her hurrying away, avoiding him? He might think she was yet another person who assumed he was a criminal.

She stepped round a tangle of Michaelmas daisies

so that he could see her. 'Hi, Luke,' she managed to say in a reasonably normal voice.

He turned sharply and stopped swinging as her feet rustled through leaves. She wondered who he had been expecting.

'Oh – hi, Ellie.'

'Amanda said you weren't going to be here.'

'Well, I wasn't. But now I am.'

He sat looking at her, starting to swing again, gently. She didn't know what else to say. She stood awkwardly for a moment, then sat on the grass next to the cat and sipped her lemonade.

'This swing,' Luke said. 'My dad put it up for me when I was about five. There was a sand-pit as well. I used to spend hours down here. The garden seemed enormous then.'

Ellie wondered whether he'd told her this in case she thought he was peculiar to be sitting by himself on a child's swing. She hadn't realised this had been Luke's special place, as well as her own and Amanda's.

'You were here that night, weren't you?' he said, as if remembering for the first time. 'You must have wondered what the hell was going on.'

'Yes. It must have been awful for you.'

'It wasn't a lot of fun.'

'Amanda said they shut you up in a cell.'

'Yes, they did.'

'A real cell, like in prison?' Ellie couldn't imagine it.

Luke nodded. 'Down below the police offices in a sort of cellar. Just a bare cell with a bunk and a bog, and graffiti all over the walls. It was bloody cold down there but the blankets were so filthy I didn't fancy using them. When it got to about three in the morning I started to think I'd never get out. It felt like being in Turkey or South America or somewhere – you know how people just disappear? You know the Amnesty International adverts?'

'Yes,' Ellie said. She had seen the full-page advertisements and had sometimes read them, sickened by the things people could do to each other.

'I expect that sounds melodramatic,' Luke said, scuffing a foot into the bare earth under the swing. 'But that's what it felt like.'

'And they just *left* you there?'

'No,' Luke said. 'There was a WPC down there and she was all right – treated me as if I were human, at least. She came round every half hour and brought me mugs of tea and told me what was going on. That bearded guy – the one who came round here – had got permission to keep me there while they interviewed someone else who'd been hauled in. They made me hand over my shoes and my belt – in case I tried to hang myself with it, I suppose – and everything that was in my pockets. And they gave me a piece of paper about my rights. My *rights*,' Luke repeated, fiercely. 'Never mind about my rights to be listened to.'

'But didn't they question you first? Didn't they believe you?'

'That bearded guy had it in for me from the start. I'd been seen at the sports centre before, he said, and that was enough to convince him. He shouted at me, *"You did it, didn't you? I know you did it. Why don't you admit it?"* As if he could bully me into saying *"Yeah all right, if that's what you want"*. He kept on and on at me for about an hour.'

'What did you do?'

'Stuck to my version, kept saying I hadn't done anything, hadn't touched any of the cars. That only made it worse. I could hear myself, the way I sounded – arrogant, superior, like I didn't care. Looking at him like he was dirt. I did care but I wasn't going to let him see. And that made him more angry. Perhaps if I'd pleaded or cried or something he'd have been different. But I'd have been guilty all the same as far as he was concerned.'

Ellie thought of Luke's expression on the night of the arrest – hard, aloof – and remembered that she'd wondered then whether it would be taken for guilt, or nonchalance. But it wasn't Luke's fault, how he looked. He was entitled to be angry. She felt a renewed surge of anger on his behalf, and behind it a flattering glow, because she was having a real conversation with him, by herself. It doesn't matter that he's so much older than me, she thought, we're two people having a conversation. Luke's talking to me, telling me things, as if I'm someone his own age.

'What happened when they let you out?' she asked. 'Amanda says it isn't finished yet.'

'No, it's not. They gave me a bail sheet and told me it might go to the Magistrates' Court.'

'So could you end up getting a fine,' Ellie said, 'or—'

She didn't like to say, 'Or even be sent to prison,' because it seemed so impossible. She didn't know how Luke could sit here discussing it so calmly if he really did face such awful injustice.

'I suppose so,' Luke said, 'though I don't see how they could get together enough evidence.'

'When will you find out? If you've got to go to Court?'

The cat stretched and walked towards Luke, rolling over by his feet. Luke stooped to rub its fur. 'Couple of weeks, maybe longer. And they can call me in any time they fancy, for more questioning, even if I'm at school. It makes it a bit difficult to concentrate, knowing that a squad car could come roaring up and I could be dragged off in front of everyone. What makes it worse is that most people in my year assume I did it. Think it's a bit of a laugh.'

Ellie watched as the cat stretched and clenched its claws in rhythm with its purring. She knew that it wasn't only people in Luke's year, but she didn't say so.

'They think I'm Jack the Lad all of a sudden and might get away with it if I'm lucky. It's true what they say about mud sticking, I've learned that over the last week. They think I've got a hoard of car radios stashed away somewhere and I'll start flogging them off when the dust dies down. They wouldn't find it quite such a joke,' Luke said bitterly, 'if it was them who might end up with a police record. That's what I'm worried about. That won't look too good on my references when I apply for courses or jobs.'

'Even if you're not guilty?'

'It's possible, isn't it?' Luke said.

Ellie didn't know. 'I still don't understand how it can have *happened*.'

Luke looked at her. 'It happened,' he said, 'because I'm eighteen and male. When you're an eighteen-year-old bloke, and you're not actually at work or school, a lot of people assume you're a thug, a hooligan, a delinquent, whatever they want to call it. Just being somewhere looks threatening, if people want to see it that way. You must be up to no good. God knows what it's like if you're eighteen and male and *black*,' he added savagely. 'That bearded cop wants to get someone for all the recent thefts, and I'll do as well as anyone else. Especially as I was seen with Andy, even though he had nothing to do with it. I'm surprised they didn't try to lay a charge of drug-dealing on me as well. I was in the wrong place at the wrong time, that's all.'

The cat suddenly rolled on to its feet and trotted off towards the house. Luke sat up and stretched. 'Sorry about all this whingeing.' He gave Ellie one of his rare smiles. 'Thanks for listening, anyway.'

'I don't mind,' Ellie said promptly. Of *course* she didn't mind; she wanted to go on sitting here looking at him, listening to him, missing lunch if necessary.

But Luke stood up. 'Come on. Let's go in and see if lunch is ready.'

Amanda and Bill were indoors laying the table. Amanda looked at Ellie suspiciously when she and Luke came in from the garden, but she said nothing until after the meal, upstairs in her room.

'What were you and Luke talking about, all that time?'

'Oh—' Ellie wanted to keep it private, but she said, 'He told me what happened at the police station. About the questioning and being shut in a cell.'

'Did he?' Amanda looked surprised. 'He didn't say anything about Rachel, I suppose?'

'No! Why?'

''Cos he's completely clammed up, about dumping her. Won't say a word about it. Poor old Rachel's always ringing up and he won't even speak to her. Mum says he's not being fair.'

Walking home much later, Ellie relived her conversation with Luke. It was a private treasure to be taken out and turned over and gloried in. She could remember every single thing Luke had said, how he had looked. Her own responses seemed totally inadequate, now that she thought of all the far cleverer things she could have said to show that she understood how he felt. Understood better than Rachel, perhaps? Ellie could sympathise, but overwhelming and outshining everything else was the fact that Luke had talked to her when he wouldn't talk to Rachel.

'Did you have a good time?' Mum asked when Ellie got in. They were still edging round each other cautiously since their row last weekend.

'It was great, thanks,' Ellie said, and went into the lounge to play with Becky before bedtime.

Runaway

Judith approached Ellie on the way to registration on Monday morning.

'I didn't find my headcollar,' Judith said, surreptitiously. 'And Karen – you know, who owns that Welsh cob? – told me she had a pair of reins missing as well, and someone else had lost some stirrups. There's definitely someone nicking stuff from the stables!'

'Did you report it?' Ellie asked.

'Yes. Actually I'm glad in a way about the other missing things, because now Mum and Dad know it's not my fault.'

'It's someone's, though,' Ellie said uncomfortably. 'Who? Surely the livery owners wouldn't take stuff from each other.'

'Mum and Dad are going to get me a trunk with a lock,' Judith said.

Well, fine if you've got the money, Ellie thought.

But that didn't solve the problem for everyone else.

In Art that afternoon, when Ellie returned to her place after sharpening her pencils, she found a folded piece of card on her bag. She stooped to open it and read ELLIE in Celtic lettering, with twining loops and serpents, just like Greg's own illustrated name card. Typical Greg – he was too indirect to give it to her personally. She looked across at him, and he caught her eye and flushed scarlet. He tried to hide it by turning away to take off his glasses and rub them on his sweatshirt. She knew better than to speak to him while anyone else could hear, but at the end of the lesson she waited so that they could walk across to RE together.

'Thank you – it's lovely,' she told him. 'I ought to have a better name, really, didn't I, to suit it? Like a Welsh or Irish name, from a legend – I don't know – Blodwyn, or something.'

'Or Gronya,' he said. 'That's a name from a legend.' She thought he said Gronya, but then he spelled it out for her – GRAINNE.

'Who's Grainne?' she asked, and Greg told her the story, all the way down to the RE mobiles, about Grainne running off with Diarmuid the warrior and then Diarmuid being killed by a poisonous bristle from a boar. It was quite amazing, the things he knew.

'Batman fancies you,' Amanda accused her, later.

'Don't be daft. 'Course he doesn't,' Ellie lied, feeling herself colouring up. 'He's too intellectual for that sort of thing.'

'Oh, yeah? P'raps he thinks *you're* intellectual,' Amanda teased.

Ellie just humphed, and opened a packet of crisps. It was lunchtime, and they were eating in the form-room without Natalie for once. Natalie had been given a lunchtime detention by Mrs Reynolds for having her mobile phone switched on during French, answering it when it rang, then refusing to hand it over to Ms Aronson. Mrs Reynolds wasn't impressed by Natalie's excuse that her sister Lisa needed to tell her something desperately important – there was a rule about mobile phones, and Natalie had broken it.

''Course, I could tell old Bats-in-the-Belfry he's wasting his time,' Amanda teased. 'You haven't got eyes for anyone but Luke. Specially after your cosy little chat on Sunday.'

There was no point trying to deny it. Ellie thought about Luke constantly, so much so that she'd completely missed Mr O'Shaughnessy's explanation about vectors and had no idea how to do her Maths homework. In her wilder fantasies, she pictured herself visiting Luke in prison, waiting faithfully for him to be released and earning his undying gratitude.

She longed to know what was going on, but she

didn't even see Luke that week. Amanda reported that Luke spent every evening in his room by himself. Rachel came round, twice, Amanda said, but Luke wouldn't even come down to see her.

'The second time, she cried,' Amanda reported. 'Mum had to dole out tissues and sympathy.'

Poor Rachel, Ellie thought, remembering the distraught figure stumbling blindly across the field. Poor Luke. Ellie felt totally caught up in the drama at Amanda's house, or rather lack of drama, since nothing more seemed to be happening on the police front. But that must make it worse for Luke, preparing for his mock A-Levels as if nothing out of the ordinary were going on, all the time wondering whether he'd be hauled away by police or summoned to court.

Ellie made such a mess of her maths that Mr O'Shaughnessy kept her in during Friday lunchtime to do it again. Fortunately it was only a lunchtime detention, so she didn't have to tell Mum and Dad, but the ignominy of the occasion was increased by sharing the punishment with daft little Jamie Day who got so many detentions that he had to list them in his homework diary for a fortnight ahead, like business appointments.

'*Listen*, next time I'm explaining something new,' Mr O'Shaughnessy said cuttingly when she handed in her book. 'I could tell you were miles away on some other planet, but perhaps you could revisit Earth just occasionally, for Maths lessons at least?'

The thefts at the riding school continued to worry Ellie, as well as her other preoccupations. Judith, who went there on Thursday evenings to ride Florian, told her on Friday that someone had reported a missing sweat rug. Things were disappearing far too often to be explained away as an outbreak of carelessness among the livery owners.

On Saturday, after Ellie's lesson, Frances looked over the door of Freddie's stable where she was unsaddling, and said, 'Sue and Nigel want to see you up at the house. Can you go straight round there when you've done that?'

'Me? What for?' Ellie called out, but Frances was already gone.

Apprehension nibbled at Ellie's stomach as she put Freddie's tack away, taking time to arrange the stirrup leathers and thread the reins through the throat lash and even to give the bit a quick clean. She could only think of one reason for Nigel and Sue wanting to see her at the house and that was that they suspected her of the thieving. Otherwise why wouldn't Frances have passed on whatever they wanted to tell her?

She walked slowly along the path that passed between rows of conifers and led to the Hunts' private area. When Mrs Charwelton lived here she often invited Ellie and Amanda in for orange squash and biscuits, but Ellie hadn't been in since the Hunts' arrival. The ivy that had scrambled over the porch had been stripped off and the brickwork repointed, and Mrs Charwelton's tangle of cottagey plants had been replaced by dwarf conifers, heather and gravel. Ellie had liked it better as it was before.

What was she going to say? They thought she was a suspect, like Luke. They were going to accuse her. She was guilty of being in the wrong place at the wrong time. She was in and out of the livery tack-room all the time; she knew what was stored in there and could easily nip in at lunchtime when there was no one around. Perhaps they had already told the police about her. Maybe her name was on a list of suspicious characters, next to Luke's. So this was how it felt, to be wrongly blamed. People would look at you with accusing eyes, and their suspicion would make you start to believe it yourself. You'd start to doubt that you knew what you had or hadn't done. You could have stolen things absent-mindedly, without noticing. And whatever you said, however much you protested, it would sound like lying, even to yourself. Ellie's feet dragged. At the very least, Nigel and Sue wouldn't want her at the stables any more. They were going to tell her to go away and not to come back. Wouldn't it be easier just to go, without seeing them?

But she was nearly there now. It felt worse than being sent to the Year Head. The back door was open and Sue and Nigel Hunt were in the extended kitchen, drinking coffee at the breakfast bar, their long thoroughbred legs stretched out. They were both dressed ready to ride and Nigel was flicking through *Horse and Hound*. The kitchen was very tidy, every surface clear. In Mrs Charwelton's day there would have been a heap of snoring dogs in a basket and a muddle of show entry forms and bits of saddlery all over the table, so that you'd have to shove the clutter aside to put down a mug of tea. Ellie went in, reluctantly.

'Oh, hi, Ellie,' Sue said, smiling at her. 'Thanks for coming round. Have some coffee?'

Ellie was so taken aback that she said yes, even though she didn't usually drink coffee, especially not strong filter stuff. What was this, a softening-up process before they went in for the kill?

Sue poured coffee from a jug on a hotplate. She had smooth blonde hair brushed back under a headband and a slim figure that looked good in riding clothes; she was the sort of person who never looked hot or untidy. 'Milk? Sugar?' She smiled at Ellie again as she handed her the cup, and Nigel put down the *Horse and Hound*.

'We want to put something to you, Ellie,' he said.

'We know what a lot of good work you do around the yard, and how reliable and capable you are.'

Definitely softening-up. Ellie stared at him, wondering why he didn't get straight to the point. Neither Nigel nor Sue had ever taken so much notice of her before.

'Frances and Paula both speak very highly of you,' Sue said. 'You're an enormous help, especially on our busy Saturdays. The point is that we'd like to pay you for what you do and make it a more formal arrangement. We can give you ten pounds for the day and you needn't pay anything for your lesson. If you agree, there's a form for you to fill in for insurance purposes and we'd need your parents to sign. What do you think? Does that sound like a good idea?'

Ellie made a rapid mental adjustment. 'Yes, it does. Thank you.'

'We realise you might not be able to make *every* Saturday,' Nigel continued. 'Frances said you had something else on last week. But if you can let Frances know in advance, that'll be fine.'

'Paula says you're a good little rider, as well,' Sue said. 'She says you've come on no end. We'll have to build on that. Move you up to horses – you're quite a lightweight, but tall. I don't see why you couldn't ride Taurus, for example.'

'*Could* I? That'd be great!'

'Why not? Perhaps we'll even put you in one of the adult intermediate lessons.'

Ellie was beginning to feel light-headed. She wasn't used to receiving such lavish praise. She took the form from Sue, thanked her again and was about to go back to the yard when Nigel said, 'There is something else. Something less pleasant, I'm afraid. I don't know whether you've heard about the thefts from the livery tack-room?'

'Yes, I have,' Ellie said. At least now she could be reasonably confident they weren't going to accuse her – not after offering her a job. 'Judith told me.'

'We're going to have to be careful,' Nigel said, 'about locking up at lunchtimes and keeping a general eye on things. And do let us know if you see anyone strange hanging around the place.'

Hanging around.

'Yes, OK,' Ellie said doubtfully. People didn't hang around, they came quite legitimately to ride out or have a lesson or wait for someone.

'The odd thing is,' Sue said, 'it's only small items that are disappearing. It's obviously not serious tack thieves or they'd have taken the saddles – there are at least two Stübben saddles in there, worth a lot of money. This is more like someone picking up odd things that are lying around. Anyway, keep your eyes open, won't you?'

Ellie said she would. Nigel picked up the *Horse and Hound* again, which seemed to mean that the interview was over, and Ellie went back to the yard, almost skipping. Apart from the worry about the thefts, she felt buoyant with happiness and relief. It bubbled and fizzed inside her, hardly containable. Far from being a suspect, she was reliable, responsible, an enormous help. A good little rider! And even *Frances* had said nice things about her! Typical, not to say them to my face, she thought. But when she passed Frances on her way round to the pony barn, Frances stopped and said, 'All sorted out, then?'

'Yes, thanks.'

'Good. We wouldn't want you to drift off the way Amanda has. You're a great help.' As if surprised to find herself saying so much, Frances nodded curtly, said, 'Don't forget to check the hay-nets in the pony barn, will you?' and went on her way.

Ellie was beginning to think this was the sort of day when nothing could go wrong. And not just today – some nice things had happened over the last week, as well as the problems. Getting over her row with Mum, being good friends with Amanda again, talking to Luke—

And then she felt guilty for feeling so happy when the threat of the Magistrates' Court was still hanging over Luke. How could she have forgotten, even for a moment?

Going in for History on Tuesday, Ellie followed Judith into the room and looked at Judith's impeccably neat French plait, thinking how typical it was of Judith. French plaits were done in exactly the same way that you did a pony's tail for a show, but ponies' tails were bristlier and strands kept escaping; Ellie had tried to do it on Freddie and had found herself in need of a third hand to do it successfully. She wondered whether Judith did her plait herself. She gave the impression of being quick and neat, good at fiddly things. Judith went to the front of the classroom where she sat next to Samantha Warburton. The pair of them always sat in faintly martyred silence through the antics of the Wishart-baiters. We're far too patient, Ellie thought. When you counted up, the reasonable people in the class outnumbered the silly ones. But the troublesome faction made so much noise and fuss that they seemed like five times the number of people they actually were.

Mr Wishart started today by collecting in the homework. Jamie handed in a splodgy mess which he'd been proudly exhibiting to the back row, and Natalie hadn't got hers at all. For Mr Wishart, she didn't bother with a last-minute copying job before registration. She didn't even bother with excuses. She just said straight out, 'I haven't done it.'

'That's the third time running,' Mr Wishart snapped. 'This really won't do. I don't know how you've got the nerve to turn up without it *again*. You'll have to stay in at break.'

'I'm not staying in,' Natalie muttered, as he moved up the rows of desks.

This time, Mr Wishart didn't pretend to be conveniently deaf, the way he sometimes did. He turned round abruptly and retorted, 'What did you say?'

'I said I'm not staying in at break,' Natalie repeated clearly.

There was a fidget of anticipation in the back row as the boys looked forward to a clash of wills and a delay to the start of work. Judith turned round to look, rolling her eyes up in a *Here we go again* expression and grimacing at Ellie, who felt emboldened to say, 'Shut up, Natalie. Some of us want to get on with the lesson.'

'Ooh, listen to Miss Goody Two Shoes,' Natalie mocked. 'She wants to get on with the lesson,' she mimicked, in a smarmy little-girl voice.

Mr Wishart slapped an exercise book against the desk to remind Natalie that she was supposed to be listening to him. 'I'm not wasting time arguing about it now, Natalie,' he said shortly. 'I'll speak to you at the end of the lesson.'

'No you won't. I'm getting my mum up here,' Natalie threatened. 'She's had enough of you picking on me.'

Although he had gone a bit red in the face, Mr Wishart said quite calmly, 'Yes, please do invite your mother in. I'd be delighted to meet her.'

The boys laughed, at Natalie this time rather than at the teacher, who had scored a point off her for once. Natalie didn't like it. 'You'll meet her all right,' she muttered.

Apart from whispering ostentatiously to Amanda, Natalie did no more to interrupt the lesson. They were watching a film today about the Home Front in the First World War, which showed old-fashioned newsreel clips of all the different jobs people did. Ellie tried to ignore the tedious running commentary from Natalie, who was only interested in how ridiculous the women looked in their Land Girl outfits or in turbans and overalls for delivering coal. What did she expect them to wear, Ellie wondered – catwalk fashions?

At the end of the lesson Natalie tried to join in the headlong rush for the door which Mr Wishart still hadn't learned to prevent, but he forestalled her by getting to the door first and catching hold of her elbow. 'Not so fast, Natalie,' he said. 'Don't forget our break-time arrangement.'

'Let go of me,' Natalie said through gritted teeth.

Mr Wishart released her arm and backed off. It was raining outside and the form group who registered in the History classroom were waiting to come in, so he beckoned to Natalie to follow him into the small History office next door. After a bit of huffing, she went.

Amanda pulled a face. 'Better wait, I suppose.'

'I'm not,' Ellie said. 'If she wants to get herself into trouble and miss break, it's up to her. I didn't make all that fuss when Mr O'Shaughnessy kept me in, did I? Come on, let's go.'

After break, she and Amanda went off to their separate French groups. Natalie didn't turn up to Ms Aronson's lesson. Ellie pointed out her absence to Jo, but all Jo said was, 'Shame. I don't know how we'll get through the lesson without her.'

Ellie wondered briefly whether Mr Wishart had had the sense at last to take her to Mrs Rawlings or Mrs Dar – it was about time he did *something* – but then she thought no more about it until Amanda confronted her and Jo in a state of high agitation as they walked back to the form-room.

'Natalie's gone home!'

'Well, what's so amazing about that?'

'You didn't *see* her.' Amanda was bursting with information, full of the importance of having news to impart. 'She was in a right state. Really upset!'

Ellie slowed down. This *was* surprising. Natalie wasn't the sort of person who got upset, not about school or teachers. Ellie herself might have shed a remorseful tear if she'd been on the end of a real wigging from Mrs Dar, who could make you feel like some loathsome form of insect life if you got on the wrong side of her. But Natalie would be more likely to react with a show of wounded innocence.

'Why? What happened?' she asked.

'I don't know. She wouldn't say. She ran off across the field.'

'Stung by another wasp, I hope. Or preferably a whole swarm,' Jo said callously, and went off to join Lynette.

'Does anyone know she's gone?' Ellie asked. If you left school during the day you were supposed to sign out at reception, but Natalie probably wouldn't have bothered with that under any circumstances, least of all if she'd got herself worked up about something.

'I shouldn't think so. I bet it's something to do with Wishart,' Amanda said. 'He's always had it in for her.'

Ellie couldn't quite share Amanda's outrage. 'Oh,

come on. Whatever happened, she's been asking for it for ages. If Natalie doesn't do her homework, what does she expect? Do you think we ought to find Mr Kershaw?' she suggested.

Amanda shook her head. 'Not till we know where she's gone. I don't want to get her in more trouble. Let's go to the pay-phone and see if she's at home.'

'Why are you sticking up for her?' Ellie asked curiously. 'I thought you were off Natalie, since we went out with her and those yobs?'

'I'm not off *Natalie*,' Amanda said. 'It's Sophie and Lee and Jonno I don't like. Natalie's all right.'

Ellie found it hard to follow Amanda's switches of loyalty, but she went with her to the pay-phone in the main entrance. This was a busy thoroughfare at break-times, not the place for a private conversation, but Ellie knew that Amanda would only fret until she found out what had happened. Amanda had Natalie's phone number written in her homework diary. She keyed it in while Ellie waited.

'What? Are you all right? Why can't you tell me now?' she heard Amanda saying, and then, 'All right, then. About quarter to four.' Ringing off, Amanda put her diary and purse away in her bag with playing-for-time slowness.

'Well? What did she say?' Ellie asked impatiently.

Amanda straightened up, her face serious, puzzled.

'She wouldn't tell me. She wants me to go round after school. She says something's happened, but she wouldn't tell me over the phone.'

Rumours

Next morning, Amanda was waiting on her own under the chestnut tree. The branches were almost bare, the ground beneath littered with crispy brown leaves and empty conker shells.

'Natalie's not coming,' Amanda told Ellie, with a sidelong look that suggested there was more to tell if she chose to.

'Why? What's wrong with her?' Ellie had thought that Amanda might ring her last night after visiting Natalie, but there had been no phone call.

'Her mum was up at school last night, after we'd gone home.'

'Something to do with Mr Wishart?' Ellie guessed. It wasn't really all that awful, then, if Natalie's mum had only gone in to complain about Natalie being picked on. They wouldn't get far with the strict Deputy Head who dealt with matters of discipline.

Amanda nodded. 'He's definitely gone too far this time.'

'Mr *Wishart* has?' Ellie said. She thought it was Natalie who had gone too far. 'Why, what did he do?'

'Only assaulted her, that's all,' Amanda said with relish.

'Oh, you're joking!'

Amanda looked at Ellie sternly. 'Would I joke about something like that? This is *serious*.'

'What do you mean, assaulted her?' Ellie demanded. She couldn't begin to imagine it. 'That could mean all sorts of things.'

'You know when he took her in the office? He got between her and the door so that she couldn't get out. She refused to speak to him, just kept staring out of the window, and he got so mad that he grabbed hold of her arm and shoved her against the filing cabinet. She hit her elbow on the cabinet and she's got a big bruise on her arm where he grabbed her. She showed me. Natalie says her parents are going to sue for assault.'

'You're saying he attacked her in the History office at break, with the classroom next door full of Year Eights?'

'We both saw him take her in there, didn't we?'

'Yes, to tell her off! I don't suppose he was planning to attack her. It was hardly an assault, anyway! He must have lost his temper.'

'Exactly! Why are you making excuses for him!' Amanda retorted. 'That's bad enough, isn't it, losing his temper? Teachers aren't allowed to push and shove people. You know how hopeless he is at telling people off, and how she winds him up. Nothing he could *say* to her would make any difference. He lost his rag.'

'But if she provoked him into it—'

'So what if she did? He still did it! If all the teachers went round beating up everyone who annoys them, there'd be hundreds of kids limping about with bandages and crutches! They're not allowed to do it. It's as simple as that.'

'And he really hurt her?' Ellie asked.

'Well, what do you think! How'd you like someone grabbing your arm so hard that it made a bruise and then ramming you against a filing cabinet?'

'What will happen now?' Ellie asked morbidly.

'He'll get the sack, it's obvious. Good job too, if you ask me. He was useless.'

Ellie noticed the past tense.

'Is it really as drastic as that?' she said. 'Will he lose his job because of losing his temper for one minute? I bet he regretted it as soon as he did it. Can't he apologise to Natalie or something?'

Amanda huffed. 'Not if Natalie's parents sue him for assault. He can't just say *sorry*. You really don't realise what a slimeball he is, do you? We all saw him grab Natalie's arm in the classroom. He was well out of order.'

Ellie puzzled over the situation. 'OK,' she said, 'it was wrong and silly of him to grab hold of her, but Natalie practically made him do it, didn't she? You know how she is. The way she jeers at him and makes him look stupid in front of everyone and doesn't give him a chance. That must be hard to take, three times a week, especially when you're a new teacher. You know how she flounces about and pulls faces and mutters things he's meant to overhear. It's...' She searched her brain for the right word. 'Contemptuous.'

'I told you, that makes no difference! Natalie's only fourteen, she's a school child, even though she looks and acts much older, and Mr Wishart's a teacher! He's supposed to be responsible, a professional! Professionals don't rough people up. It doesn't matter what she did. He's in the wrong.'

Ellie had to concede this. In registration it was all round the form, wildly exaggerated. The boys clustered eagerly.

'Is it true Wishart's been sacked?'

'We always knew he was a perv.'

'He'll probably get sent to prison. He'll be able to pal up with your brother, 'Manda.'

'Oh, *shut up*, Reado—'

'What'll happen in History now, then? Haven't we got a teacher?'

'Won't make much difference. He was useless anyway.'

Some people were like vultures, Ellie thought, flocking in to pick over the bones of a juicy scandal. They were excited, not concerned. Not even really concerned about Natalie.

'Sir, is Mr Wishart here today?' Damien asked.

But Mr Kershaw, usually willing to spend registration time in general chat, was busying himself with paperwork at the desk, pretending not to hear. Until now, Ellie hadn't altogether believed that Amanda's story could be true, but Mr Kershaw's obvious avoidance of the subject convinced her. After lunch, when they were due for a History lesson, they found Mrs Dar standing at the front of the classroom with a supply teacher.

'Mr Wishart's not here today,' she said, in a tone of voice which meant *Subject not open for discussion*. 'Mr Finningley's taking the class today. I want you to work from the textbook and answer the questions on pages 56 and 57. Mr Finningley will be able to help you if you're stuck.' She waited until the books were handed out and everyone was working in silence before nodding to Mr Finningley and leaving. Mr Finningley was an experienced ex-teacher and a regular stand-in; he wasn't going to allow chatter or speculation. Ellie glanced at the textbook and saw that it was really just a comprehension exercise, answering simple questions from the previous few pages. It dealt with stuff they'd done in class already. Mr Wishart had been going to tell them about Siegfried Sassoon throwing his Military Cross medal in the River Mersey, which would have been far more interesting. Ellie couldn't concentrate, her mind buzzing with conflicting ideas and questions. Where was Mr Wishart now? Surely he couldn't be sacked as quickly as that? Had he been suspended, like a naughty pupil, or was he being questioned by the police? Something serious *had* happened, that much was clear; Mrs Dar hadn't said anything about Mr Wishart being ill, or coming back after half-term with their marked work.

Ellie couldn't share the boys' mood of suppressed excitement. All day long the subject was rolled to and fro, like a snowball gathering snow until it was too enormous to handle. Ellie didn't want to hear any more. She wanted to leave it alone. She wanted it not to have happened. She had felt sorry for Mr Wishart; she had tried to encourage him by doing her best work, and now he had let her down.

'I suppose we'll never find out what happens to him,' Amanda said as they walked down the driveway at the end of the day. 'It's not likely to be announced in assembly, is it, or in the next newsletter? Or do you think it will get into the papers…?'

'Do you think he's really gone, for good?' Ellie asked, in spite of her resolve to say nothing more. 'Or will he be back after half-term?'

'He'll have to go,' Amanda said, like a hanging judge pronouncing sentence. 'They couldn't let him loose in a classroom again after that.'

Ellie was glad that Luke wasn't driving them home today. He too would be affected by Mr Wishart's – crime? offence? – she didn't know what to call it – because he'd lose his A-Level teacher. She wondered whether Luke knew what had happened, and what he thought now about the teacher he'd said was brilliant.

'You kids see things in such black-and-white terms,' Dad said later, when Ellie told him and Mum about Mr Wishart's sudden disappearance. 'Of course he won't have been sacked, not just like that. There'll be procedures to go through, statements taken, that sort of thing. They can't sack people without a fair investigation. And with this sort of thing it's one person's word against another's. Difficult. From what you say about this Natalie, I wouldn't be surprised if she made the whole thing up.'

But there was Natalie's bruise, Ellie thought. That was proof, surely?

'Mr Wishart wasn't at school today,' she pointed out. 'That makes him look guilty, doesn't it? If he hadn't done anything why would he stay away?'

Dad looked at her. 'Remember how furious you were when people thought Luke was guilty, just because he'd been accused? Shouldn't this teacher get the same benefit of the doubt?'

It was half-term week, and although Ellie had been looking forward to it, the time stretched out emptily. In spite of the recent ups and downs with Amanda, she missed the daily contact; especially now, for updates on the various crises that were going on in the background. Amanda and her family, including Luke, had gone to the Lake District for a few days.

Ellie was pleased when Frances suggested that she might put in extra hours at the stables if she were free, as there were more lessons than usual during the school holiday. Late on Thursday afternoon, Ellie was carrying hay-nets round to the livery yard when she heard the clatter of hooves approaching fast. Florian trotted round the corner, riderless, reins dangling; he was breathing hard, sweat darkening his neck and flanks. Ellie had seen Judith ride out about an hour earlier. She must have had a fall – maybe she was lying injured somewhere. Ellie caught hold of Florian's bridle and led him into his stable, adjusting the reins so that he couldn't tread on them, then hurried round to the main yard to tell someone.

Frances was grooming Spanish Ledge. 'Quickest thing would be if I got on Florian and went to look for her,' she said when Ellie explained. They went back to Florian's stable and Ellie led him out and checked his girth, but before Frances could mount, Judith appeared round the corner of the stable block, her face dirty and tear-stained. She had mud down one side of her jodhpurs and was limping. Frances let go of Florian's reins and went over to her.

'You OK? What happened?'

'I fell off,' Judith explained unnecessarily. 'He was fussing and fidgeting about - you know how he does.' She looked at Ellie. 'And then a pheasant flew up from the long grass, right under his nose, and he shied and bolted. I just couldn't stop him. I thought we'd gallop all the way back here. Then he swerved round a tree and I crashed off.'

'Hurt yourself?' Frances asked.

Judith rubbed her thigh. 'Just banged my leg. Nothing serious. I was terrified, though.' Her eyes filled with tears and she bent to brush the mud off her jodhpurs.

Frances went back to Florian and looked him over for injury. 'He seems all right. Lucky he came straight back here and didn't gallop across the main road.

Here you are, then.' She held the reins out to Judith. 'Best thing you can do is get back on him and ride quietly in the school for half an hour.'

Judith shook her head. 'I can't. I still feel sick.'

'You know what they say you should do after a fall. Get straight back in the saddle. This pony needs calming down, too.'

'No.' Judith sounded obstinate. 'I'm not getting on him again. Not today.' She looked at Ellie. 'You can ride him. You'd do that for me, wouldn't you?'

Ellie hesitated. She knew that the point was for Judith to get her confidence back by riding the pony herself, not for someone else to do it. She looked at Frances, who nodded and said, 'All right, then. Just quietly in the school, Ellie, for ten minutes or so. *Then* Judith can take over.'

Ellie led Florian into the school and mounted, settling herself in the lovely cushiony saddle and trying not to feel too excited. She had longed to ride him ever since he had arrived, but she would prefer it not to have happened this way, with Judith watching from the gallery. Florian was beautiful to ride, as she had expected, long-striding and responsive. He was tense and nervy at first, but soon settled, arching his neck to her touch on the reins as she trotted him steadily in circles and figure-eights. After a while, Frances appeared through the sliding doors, and said,

'That's fine, Ellie. Try a canter now.'

Ellie pushed on and Florian responded eagerly. Oh, he was her dream pony! If it really were a dream, Judith would hand him over to her to ride in all the shows and would watch admiringly as Ellie jumped beautiful clear rounds... Ellie knew she was riding well, confidently. Florian was the sort of pony who *made* you ride well.

'OK then, that'll do. Judith, your turn.' Frances came up close to pat the pony's neck. 'He and Judith are a pretty disastrous combination, I'm afraid,' she said in an undertone. 'She'll spoil him at this rate. You'd get on with him fine.'

Amanda and her family came home from the Lake District that day, and in the evening Amanda came round to see Ellie. Ellie was longing to talk about her ride on Florian, but Amanda had far more important news.

'It's all right about Luke! They're not going to bring charges after all.'

'Really?' Ellie said, in a daze of confusion about how things worked where police were concerned.

'We'd only just got in when two policemen came round to tell him. He won't have a police record, which is what he was worried about – his name's been cleared, and they think they've got someone else for nicking the radios. But Bill's still furious about the way they treated Luke. You know he put in an official complaint? That's still being looked into, and one of the policemen who came round told us that in his opinion the whole business had been completely mishandled. He did say about five times that it was only his opinion, though. Nothing official.'

'You mean, they can haul you in and threaten you and lock you up in a cell and then not even apologise when they've got it all wrong?' Ellie said.

'Well, we don't really know till we hear about the official enquiry. Maybe there'll be an apology then. There ought to be.'

Ellie thought of what Luke had said about mud sticking. It wasn't simply a matter of wiping the slate clean, pretending nothing had happened. It wasn't something Luke could easily forget, being treated as guilty.

'So Luke's looking a lot happier now,' Amanda continued, 'especially as he's made up with Rachel as well.'

'Oh?' Ellie thought she could actually hear her heart thumping in her chest. 'When?'

'It was all quite romantic really. For the first couple of days, Mum and Bill and I went on boat trips and walked round lakes and all that sort of stuff, and Luke went mooning about by himself. Then suddenly he was demanding everyone's change and spending hours on the phone. And next day Rachel came up to Windermere by train.'

'And then what?'

Amanda giggled. 'Well, we all had to be awfully tactful. They disappeared for the evening and Luke came back late. Rachel couldn't stay at our B & B place 'cos it was full, so she booked in at the Grasmere Youth Hostel. Yesterday morning Luke went to meet her there, early, and they spent all day together, walking up Helvellyn. Or at least, that's what they said they'd been doing. When they came back, you could tell everything was all right again.'

Ellie imagined herself as Rachel, walking hand-in-hand with Luke in the Lake District hills, and thought that even riding Florian would pale into insignifance, compared to that. She tried to be pleased, for Luke, for both of them. Really, she felt heavy with dejection at the crushing of her fantasies, in which she was the only person who could understand Luke and comfort him, in spite of the age difference. It had been once only, that conversation by the swing tree. She had been ready to listen when he needed someone, that was all.

Fantasy World

By the last Saturday of half-term, the last warm days of autumn had given way to blustery rain and chill winds. After the usual riding lesson, Amanda left to catch the bus home; she was going shopping with her mother in the afternoon. Ellie helped Paula with the children's lesson and the midday feeds, and the yard quietened down for lunchtime.

Now that it was too cold to stay outside, Ellie usually ate her sandwiches in the tack-room, where there was a heater and a kettle. She made herself a mug of tea and was settling into the leather-smelling warmth when she remembered that Frances had asked her to bring in Glendower, the Welsh cob, from the paddock; his owner was coming to ride him later and he'd need time to dry off. Ellie pulled on her waterproof and collected a headcollar, and went down towards the paddock gate. She hurried head-down against the cold rain but as she passed the end of the livery yard her eye was caught by a sudden movement. Someone was there, darting away from the locked tack-room door – Ellie had a swift impression of short dark hair and a long fringe. And a second girl – both of them were now running to the gate at the far end. The farther one turned as she climbed the gate, just for a second, but long enough for Ellie to recognise her as Natalie. Natalie, with Sophie!

Ellie's heart was thumping so loudly that she could hear it pulsing in her ears. It was pointless to run after them. They were into the field, running across soaked grass towards a scrubby bit of woodland that adjoined the main road. Ellie didn't delude herself that they'd come to ask about riding lessons or to visit one of the livery owners – that would be stretching generosity too far. Sophie had definitely been trying the livery tack-room door. The Hunts had only recently started locking it at lunchtimes, and Ellie wondered how many times Sophie and Natalie had been here before, to see what was lying around.

Natalie!

In all her wonderings about the tack-thief, Ellie had never thought of Natalie. Natalie didn't know much about horses or saddlery, but Sophie did – Ellie remembered that Sophie used to come riding here. Sophie must be the one who knew how to get rid of the stuff – by selling it, presumably. Neither of them would have any use for it but the saddler in town bought and sold second-hand gear. Ellie stood there for a moment with the rain driving into her face, wondering what to do. If it had been Sophie on her own, she would have told the Hunts straight away – which she probably ought to do in any case – but because Natalie was involved, she wanted to see Amanda first.

Ellie thought of the uncharacteristic interest Natalie had shown when she'd come to the stables on those two occasions. She was probably taking note of the quietest times and where the best stuff was kept. Well, Ellie thought, I fell for that all right, didn't I? Poor little Natalie, who couldn't afford a riding lesson!

She rang Amanda as soon as she got home.

'Are you doing anything? There's something I've got to tell you.'

'I've got something to tell you too,' Amanda said. 'Can you come round? Mum!' she yelled. 'It's all right if Ellie comes round, isn't it? We're having pizza,' she added. 'Mum and Bill have been making dough all afternoon.'

When Ellie arrived they went straight upstairs to confer in Amanda's bedroom, sitting side by side on the bed.

'OK, what?' Amanda demanded.

'No, you first.' Ellie thought Amanda's news item must be to do with Luke. Natalie could take second place.

'Well.' Amanda paused for dramatic effect. 'I went round to Natalie's at lunchtime, and she wasn't there.'

No, because she was trying to nick stuff from the stables, Ellie thought, but she said, 'And?'

'Her mum was, though. She said I could go in to wait for a minute because Natalie had gone to the shops but might be back any minute'. So I did, and she gave me a Coke and we sat in the kitchen. And then she started talking about Luke. I suppose Natalie must have told her what was going on. She said, "I hear your brother's been in a bit of bother," so I told her he hadn't done anything and about the police coming round last week. She didn't even seem to hear that bit. She said, "I'm glad I never had a boy. My two girls get themselves into enough trouble as it is."' Amanda looked at Ellie significantly and repeated, '*Never had a boy*. That's what she said.'

Ellie stared back.

'Never had a—? Oh, but what about—?'

'Exactly.' Amanda nodded. 'It took me a second or two to think of that, but then I said, "Oh! I thought Natalie had a brother called Liam." No reaction. Not a flicker. Just looked at me and said, "No, I've just got the two. Natalie and Lisa. They're enough for me, I can tell you." And she *laughed*.'

Ellie was baffled. 'You don't think she could have – you know – blocked it out of her mind, about the brother? She could have done. People sometimes do that, don't they, when something awful happens?'

'But the point is, it didn't happen!' Amanda said. 'I looked at her carefully when I said it and there wasn't even a twitch of an eyelid.'

'So you mean—'

Amanda nodded again. 'Yes. Natalie made the whole thing up.'

Ellie thought this over for a few moments, recalling that she'd seen no photographs of Liam in the house, no belongings, mementoes, nothing. The notion of there ever having been a Liam came from Natalie, and then she had only told Amanda, in confidence.

'But why would she invent something like that?'

Amanda made a don't-ask-me gesture. 'To make herself sound more interesting, I suppose. And it's a pretty good way of getting sympathy whenever you want, isn't it? I was stupid to believe her, now I think about it.'

'But why shouldn't you? You wouldn't expect anyone to lie about something like that. Actually,' Ellie confessed, '*I* made up a story like that. You know, the one I had to read out in English, about the war. The boy in it – the one I called John – was really Luke.'

Amanda looked at her exasperatedly. 'That's not the same thing, though, is it? You made up a story. You didn't try to make it into real life or tell anyone it was true. Being dotty about Luke is one thing. Telling people a big lie like Natalie did is something else.'

'I s'pose.'

'You know what?' Amanda went on. 'I reckon she made it up about her mum being on the booze as well. I've been round there a few times lately and her mum's never drunk anything stronger than coffee.'

Ellie looked at her, not sure whether Amanda's thoughts were running in the same direction as hers.

'So,' Amanda said, 'it made me wonder whether she made it up about Mr Wishart, as well. She obviously lives in a fantasy world, making up all sorts of lies.'

'But – the bruise on her arm?'

Amanda shrugged. 'It's easy enough to get a bruise. I've got two big ones now – one on my leg where I bumped into the coffee table and one I got in PE. But what are we going to do about it? And what were you going to tell me?'

And Ellie remembered that she hadn't even started on the tack thefts.

When they went downstairs, some while later, Luke was in the kitchen with Bill, cutting up mushrooms, tomatoes and peppers for the pizza. The cat sat on the draining board watching as they built up colourful piles. The kitchen was full of the yeasty smell of pizza dough and the cool scent of cut peppers.

'Bill,' Amanda said, linking her arm through his. 'Why don't you and Mum sit down by the fire and have a nice drink? You must be tired after all this cooking. We'll finish the pizzas with Luke.'

Bill looked suspicious, but laughed and allowed himself to be steered out of the kitchen. 'Sounds all right to me. No olives on mine, remember, Luke. Can't stand the things.'

'What are you up to?' Luke said to Amanda, wielding a huge knife. 'You're not usually quite so considerate. I notice I'm not included.'

'Isn't Rachel coming round?' Amanda asked.

Luke looked up at the kitchen clock. 'Not yet. In about an hour.'

'Good,' Amanda said. 'We want to talk to you. On your own. It's important.'

Luke looked surprised. He glanced at Ellie. 'OK. If you help. Can one of you start spreading tomato paste on those bases? That cheese needs slicing and then goes on next.' Ellie still saw him as the hero of her story, the doomed young soldier with his beautiful blue-grey eyes shadowed by the peak of his cap. But she couldn't gaze at him too adoringly, or

Amanda would notice and start smirking.

'We know how to make pizza,' Amanda retorted. 'We've done it at school.'

Ellie was glad to have something to do while Amanda talked. Luke listened without comment while Amanda explained about the tack thefts, the fantasy brother and their doubts about the Mr Wishart affair.

'So we thought,' Amanda concluded, gazing at Luke with wide-eyed younger-sister flattery, 'you'd know what to do.'

'Hmm.' Luke considered the pattern he was making on the first of the pizzas with strips of red and green pepper. 'Well, it's difficult. It wouldn't surprise me if you're right, from what I've seen of that Natalie girl. The school governors, or whoever's dealing with it, must realise there's a chance she made it all up, but obviously she's got to be heard and taken seriously. Cases like that have to be.' He selected half a black olive and placed it carefully in the centre.

'Do *you* think he didn't do it?' Ellie said.

Luke took another olive from the jar and ate it slowly before replying. 'It would be easy enough to lose your temper and hit or shove someone on the spur of the moment. Some kids at school are so mouthy and rude, I don't know how the teachers put up with them. On the other hand, if he says he didn't and it's his word against Natalie's, I know who I'd believe.'

'But he wasn't at school next day,' Amanda said. 'Everyone thought that meant he was guilty.'

Luke glanced at her and then at Ellie, frowning. She thought of their swing tree conversation and wondered whether Luke was remembering it too.

'I wouldn't take that as proof of guilt,' Luke said. 'I can understand how he must have felt, especially if he hadn't done anything. It's horrible to know that everyone's gossiping about what you did or didn't do and what's going to happen. 'Specially for a teacher, who's got to face thirty different kids every hour of the day. And Wishart's only a young bloke, in his first year of teaching. Not all that much older than me. It must have given him quite a knock.'

'So what do you think we should do?' Amanda asked.

Luke pushed the first pizza away and began decorating a second. 'Well, if you're right, it's a serious allegation she's made, professional misconduct, and she'd better come clean. I should think the first thing you'd better do is see if you can get any sense out of her.'

Amanda looked doubtful. 'You mean, *ask* her?'

'How else?' Luke said. 'What do you like on your pizza, Ellie?'

*

Ellie and Amanda had agreed to go round to Natalie's house next morning, but when the time came Ellie would far rather have stayed at home. Becky was drawing in the kitchen and Mum ironing while she listened to the omnibus edition of *The Archers*, her Sunday morning ritual even though she usually heard most of the episodes during the week and claimed not to like it anyway. Ellie heard *The Archers* from time to time without meaning to and could recognise some of the characters by their voices – today Mrs Snell was complaining about litter on the village green. Ellie, dreading the confrontation with Natalie, would have preferred to listen to Mrs Snell and her problems until the end of the programme. Litter on the village green would be a manageable problem.

She met Amanda and they walked on down to Natalie's, which was shut up in Sunday quietness. Natalie's mum opened the door to them. She was wearing a dressing-gown and her hair was unbrushed even though it was nearly eleven. It was the first time Ellie had seen her. She was small, blonde like Natalie, with a pert face which Ellie thought could become fierce if she had to stand up for her daughter. Ellie imagined her at school in the Head's office, threatening to sue Mr Wishart.

Natalie's mum yawned. 'Christ, you're early. I

think Natalie's around somewhere. Nat!' she yelled. 'Your friends are here!'

They went up to Natalie's room. Ellie felt awful. What Luke said had sounded clear enough, 'You'll have to see if you can get any sense out of her,' and she and Amanda had agreed what they were going to say, but she was sure it wouldn't be that simple. Not with Natalie.

Natalie, wearing jeans and a sweatshirt, was sitting cross-legged on her bed eating cereal and listening to her Walkman. 'Oh, it's you two,' she said. She gave Ellie a hard, suspicious stare. Till now, Ellie hadn't been sure whether Natalie had recognised her at the stables. She knew now that Natalie had. She felt herself blushing – *why*, when Natalie ought to be the one who was ashamed?

'Natalie,' Amanda said firmly, 'we've come to ask you something.'

'Oh yeah?' Natalie slid the headphones back so that they rested round her neck.

'We know you've been nicking stuff from the stables,' Amanda said. 'But there's something else we want to know.'

'Oh, yeah?' Natalie said again. She continued eating cereal but watched them both guardedly. Ellie looked round at the luxury of Natalie's bedroom and wondered why she needed to steal. But then she didn't understand why Natalie did half the things she did.

Amanda took a deep breath. 'We want to know what really happened with Mr Wishart.'

'Oh, that,' Natalie said. 'Told you, didn't I? What d'you want to hear it all again for? I'm fed up with going over and over it, making statements. What difference does it make anyway? It looks like he's gone now, and good riddance. It worked, didn't it?'

'What do you mean, "It worked"?' Ellie said suspiciously.

Natalie gave her a scathing look. 'What is this, the Gestapo? What have you done then, up at the stables? I suppose you couldn't wait to grass on me. Well, it's only your word against mine. I haven't got the stuff any more. Sophie sold it. It was all her idea anyway. Who's going to prove anything?'

'I suppose the saddler might be able to remember Sophie going in with tack to sell,' Ellie said. She could tell from Natalie's expression that her guess was right. 'The things might still be in the shop. Anyway, we haven't done anything yet. We haven't told the Hunts or the police. And we won't, if you agree to stop doing it, and if you—'

'If you tell us what really happened with Mr Wishart,' Amanda said.

Natalie looked scornful. 'What difference does it

make? It's all sorted out now. He's cleared off. He was a bloody useless teacher and I got rid of him, didn't I? Did us all a favour.'

'OK, then, Ellie,' Amanda said, moving towards the door. 'We'd better go and tell the Hunts who's been nicking that stuff. I expect they'll call the police in.'

'Oh, all right,' Natalie said, looking alarmed for the first time. 'I did exaggerate a bit about Wishart. So what?'

'If you exaggerated it,' Ellie said, 'how did you get the bruise on your arm?'

Natalie laughed. 'Oh, that. It was Lee, while we were mucking about. I bruise easy. Came in handy, though.' She looked at Amanda. 'You fell for it all right.'

Amanda glanced at Ellie. 'So how much *did* you make up? Did he touch you at all?'

'You saw him,' Natalie said defiantly. 'He grabbed my arm and stopped me going out the door.'

'So that's *all*?' Ellie said. 'That's hardly an attack! You mean, apart from that he just took you in the office and told you off?'

Natalie turned her face away and pulled at a loose thread on the seam of her duvet. 'I was sick of him getting at me all the time. Picking on me.' It crossed Ellie's mind that she looked like a sulky child instead of the sophisticated teenager she liked to be.

'Natalie,' Amanda said, 'd'you mean to say you made it all up, about him shoving you against the cabinet and bruising your arm? You've got to go to the Head tomorrow and tell her.'

Natalie shook her head. 'No way. I'm not doing it.'

'Got the Hunts' phone number, Ellie?' Amanda said.

'I'm not doing it,' Natalie repeated. 'Look, what I'll do if you like is tell Mum I exaggerated a bit. Get her and Dad to back down. That'll have to do. I'm fed up with it all anyway.' She looked at Ellie narrowly. 'So you won't say anything about the nicking?'

'That depends,' Ellie said. 'It's not enough, getting your mum to back down. You've got to say you made it all up. Not to your mum. To someone at school.'

'No. *You* can tell them if you want.' Natalie looked at her defiantly. 'It's what you want, isn't it? They'll listen to you, Miss Goody Two Shoes. You're the sort of good little girl they want at their stupid school.'

'It's important, Natalie. It's –' Ellie found herself quoting Luke: 'a serious allegation you've made. Professional misconduct. It's more than just getting your own back on a teacher you don't like.'

'All right! I've told you – I'll back down a bit, say I was in a state and I exaggerated a bit. Finished now?

Going home to polish your haloes? She stood up and disentangled herself from the flex of the Walkman. 'I'm going out with my *friends*.'

'That was awful,' Amanda said when they got outside.

The wind rustled the trees and got into the gaps between Ellie's clothes, making her shiver and pull the zip on her coat right up to the collar. The temperature had taken a wintry plummet.

'She isn't *sorry*,' she said, 'about any of it. She doesn't understand. She made all that up and she still doesn't understand what it means for Mr Wishart, being accused like that. She still thinks it's a game. And the stealing. None of it matters to her, unless she gets caught!'

'So what do we do now?' Amanda asked. 'Anything? Or nothing?'

Ellie considered. 'Let's tell Luke. He'll know what to do.'

They walked back to Amanda's and found Luke in the drive outside the house, doing something technical and oily under the bonnet of Amanda's mum's car.

'Told you,' he said when Amanda had explained, 'I said stay away from that girl. Trouble waiting to happen, she is.'

'OK, O wise and wonderful brother,' Amanda said,

with a mock bow. 'But now what?'

Luke straightened and wiped his hands on a filthy rag. 'I don't know why you think I've got all the answers. But if I were you I'd go and see Mrs Dar. She's Mr Wishart's Head of Department and she ought to be told.'

'No,' Amanda said promptly. 'Natalie's the one who ought to tell her. I'm not doing it.'

Fireworks

'You two are in luck,' Mr Kershaw said to Ellie and Amanda at registration on Tuesday. 'Special delivery.' He held out a folded and stapled sheet of paper.

Ellie unfastened it and read, in sloping green handwriting: *Please see me in the History office at break this morning. V. Important! S. Dar.*

'Thanks a lot, Luke,' Amanda muttered.

'What's Luke got to do with it?' Ellie asked.

'He went to see her,' Amanda said. 'Because I told him I wouldn't. We talked about it again after you'd gone on Sunday. Luke said he knows we don't want to grass to a teacher but this is more important than that. So *he* went to see her, yesterday lunchtime. He told me.'

'Oh.' Ellie assimilated this raising of Luke's hero status.

'You know what Natalie's like.' Amanda spoke so quietly that Ellie almost had to lip-read. 'All she wants is to shut us up about the tack, so we won't tell the Hunts or the police. She might get her mum and dad to back off but she's not going to admit to lying. She's not brave enough, when it comes down to it.'

'With Natalie, you wonder if she realises she *is* lying,' Ellie muttered.

'All the same,' Amanda said wryly, 'I don't much fancy going for a chat with Mrs Radar. She terrifies me to death.'

'Oh, come on,' Ellie said. 'Just because she told you off once about not revising for a test. She's hardly going to bear you a grudge about that, is she?'

Natalie hadn't walked to school with Amanda and Ellie today or yesterday. She had turned up late for registration and was now pointedly avoiding them. She sat at the back of the form-room with Damien and Matthew and Jamie, making them laugh with her mimicry of the Head's welcome-back assembly. Ellie and Amanda were primly unimpressed. They knew what a good actress Natalie was, and how she used her talent. Mr Wishart hadn't been in History yesterday but for most of the form the subject was already old news; today's topic was the forthcoming Firework Night disco for Year Nine.

At break Ellie and Amanda reported to the History office. Mrs Dar was in there with a colleague, Mr

Walters, who picked up his mug of coffee and left as soon as the girls came in. Mrs Dar sat at a desk stacked with books on Nazi Germany and the Weimar Republic, a sheaf of essays stacked in front of her. She always wore smart suits and pinned her dark hair back off her face. Ellie wondered whether people ever yelled *'Paki'* at her in the street, the way they sometimes did at Sanjay. She couldn't imagine anyone daring to.

'Sit down, girls.' Mrs Dar had pulled two chairs round ready. 'Your brother said you had something you wanted to tell me,' she said to Amanda. 'I should tell you – both of you – that if it's what I think it is, then it's highly confidential and must be kept between the three of us. All right?'

'Yes.'

'Then – it's about Natalie Bayliss, if I'm right?'

Ellie and Amanda looked at each other.

'You start,' Amanda said to Ellie.

'Well—' Ellie began. 'We think Natalie made it all up about Mr Wishart. In fact she's more or less admitted it.'

'Go on.' Mrs Dar was looking at her steadily.

Ellie wasn't sure whether to tell Mrs Dar everything – about the stolen tack and the non-existent brother – but between them she and Amanda filled in most of the details. Mrs Dar listened, occasionally prompting or asking a question – not, Ellie noticed, looking particularly surprised or shocked. When they had finished, she looked thoughtfully at her notepad for a moment and then said, 'Thank you for telling me all this. Actually I knew already that Natalie had made it up, from Mr Wishart himself. But of course any complaint of that sort has to be thoroughly investigated. Young people have to be listened to, especially when they're making an accusation like this. But it's worth knowing that Natalie's admitted inventing it. To you two, at any rate. The Head and governors will take it seriously if she's been making up malicious lies. Very seriously indeed.' She looked at them, each in turn, and added, 'I'm afraid it's too late now to affect Mr Wishart's future here as a teacher.'

'Why?' Ellie could only imagine that the governors had already sacked him. If so, it seemed unbelievably harsh. Wouldn't they listen to his side of the story, believe what he said?

Mrs Dar hesitated again, then sighed and said, 'Because he's already handed in his resignation. I heard about it yesterday from the Head.'

'But why, if he hasn't done anything?' Amanda exclaimed.

Ellie thought of what Luke had said. Luke, more than anyone else, knew what it was like to be under suspicion. To have people gossiping about you, talking behind your back, enjoying the drama. She thought she could understand why Mr Wishart had resigned.

Mrs Dar doodled on her pad before replying. 'Teaching can be difficult enough, without that sort of pressure. It's a great pity. He had the makings of an excellent teacher. Yes, he had problems – most people do, when they start. But he would have got over them. Now – I doubt if he wants to go near a school ever again. He's a sensitive young man and this has given him an enormous blow to his confidence.'

It's not fair! Ellie wanted to shout out. *It can't happen like this!*

But it was happening. Had happened. Life wasn't fair.

'Can't you get him to come back?' she asked.

Mrs Dar looked up from her doodle. 'I shall try my best to persuade him. But once you leave in that sort of way it's hard to come back.'

Ellie wondered if she'd done something like that herself, once. She seemed to know what it was like.

Mrs Dar said, 'I don't think your friend Natalie fully understood what a serious thing she was doing.'

'Natalie isn't our friend,' Amanda said. 'Not any more.'

At afternoon registration, a messenger came into the form-room and said, loudly enough for everyone to hear, that Natalie was to go immediately to the Head's office. Natalie got up and went to the door with her normal cocky swagger, but turned in tthe doorway with a glare of transparent hatred in Amanda's and Ellie's direction. Unhappily, Ellie put her pencil-case into her rucksack and tried to remember what lesson she had next. Natalie was going to make her and Amanda pay for this.

The bell shrilled, and Jo nudged Ellie as she got to her feet. 'Forget about her. She's not worth it.'

Ellie wondered how much Jo understood: she couldn't know everything, but seemed to know enough. '*She* won't forget,' she said miserably. 'She's going to start picking on us now.'

We'll stick up for you, Lynette and me,' Jo said. 'Won't we, Lyn? Safety in numbers. What can she do, one against four?'

At the stables the horses were being clipped for the winter. Ellie had helped Frances with Taurus and was now brushing him down before putting his rug on. His coat where he had been clipped was like soft brown suede but his legs and saddle patch were left untouched, the colour of a glossy new conker. Short hairs flew into the air and tickled Ellie's nose as she worked. Nigel Hunt had spoken to her earlier, reminding her to keep the livery tack-room door locked at lunchtime, and Ellie had felt guilty for not telling him what she knew. At least there shouldn't be any more thefts now, and the Mr Wishart business had really been more serious – even if it had all turned out wrong – since someone's whole future had been involved, not just the minor nuisance of a lost headcollar or girth.

Ellie kept thinking of Mr Wishart: wondering where he was, what he was doing now. Did he have a girlfriend to support him? Did he regard himself as useless, after half a term of teaching? Did he feel that running away had stamped him permanently as guilty, a failure, a giver-up? Did failing once make you fail again, setting a pattern? And was it really his failure at all, or the fault of everyone involved? Ellie sighed, putting down her grooming brushes. She would never know.

Judith looked over the door. 'Paula said you were in here.'

'Nearly finished. Are you riding?'

'No.' Judith looked awkward, and Ellie saw that she wasn't dressed for riding but wore a soft white sweater with a bobble pattern, with her hair loose over her shoulders. 'That's why I was looking for you. Florian's going to be sold. He isn't the pony for me and I'd only end up spoiling him. Frances knows someone who wants to buy him, for jumping and shows. She says it's a good home.'

'Oh.' Ellie picked up Taurus' rug and unfolded it, hiding her disappointment. All the same, she knew it was best for Florian to go to an owner who could ride him properly and wasn't afraid of him.

'I know you're disappointed, Ellie. I'm sorry I couldn't give him to you – I would if I could,' Judith said matter-of-factly. 'He went so well for you and you looked so good on him. But Mum and Dad wanted to get their money back.'

'I couldn't begin to afford it anyway, keeping a pony,' Ellie said, throwing the rug over Taurus' back and pulling it straight. 'Are they going to get you another one, then?'

'No. We've decided that riding isn't really for me,' Judith said. She was already looking happier, relieved of her problem.

Ellie told herself that she didn't really mind anyway. It was just a dream, riding in shows, winning trophies. She didn't need that. She enjoyed being with the horses, looking after them, learning about them. Being treated as a responsible person.

Mrs Sutherland pulled up in the Audi and Judith said, 'Well, thanks for all your help, Ellie.'

'That's all right,' Ellie said. She would miss seeing Judith around the place. There would be no reason for her to come here any more.

'Will you be at the Year Nine disco next week?' Judith asked.

'Yes, I think so.'

'Good. See you on Monday, then.' Judith waved and went to the car. Ellie wouldn't have thought school discos were Judith's sort of thing, but then she wouldn't have thought they were Greg Batt's sort of thing either and he'd already asked if she was going.

Getting ready to go to Amanda's that evening, Ellie was side-tracked into her own back garden, where Mum and Dad were lighting sparklers in the garden for Becky. Only sparklers, because Becky would be going to a firework-and-birthday-party at a school friend's tomorrow night. Becky watched the sparklers, round-eyed, but was too frightened to hold them, even with gloves on, until Ellie held her hand over Becky's on the stick of a sparkler to show that it didn't hurt, that the dancing sparks were just flecks of light. At last Becky held one at arm's length with her face turned away, and then with more confidence, crying out in disappointment when the fizzing light sputtered and faded.

Life was simple for Becky. There was always someone there, someone bigger and wiser, to hold her hand, comfort her, guide her. Ellie knew that she shouldn't envy Becky but sometimes it was difficult not to, faced with big, unsolvable problems. You couldn't go back to childhood; there was no way back. But you didn't have to rush forward too quickly either.

After the sparklers Ellie went round to Amanda's, for fireworks and a bonfire and a barbecue. Bill and Luke had built a big bonfire and everyone went outside and gathered round as the flames gathered strength, spitting on damp twigs, consuming paper, sending golden sparks leaping. Besides the barbecue, there were potatoes roasting in their jackets at the edge of the bonfire. It was a cold, crisp night, almost frosty, and standing by the fire gave Ellie a scalded front and a chilled back.

'What you need to do is spit-roast yourself,' Amanda said, turning round slowly to demonstrate. 'Cooking each bit of yourself in turn.'

Rachel was there with Luke, though they were going on to a party somewhere else later. They stood hand-in-hand watching the flames, their faces lit gold. They spoke to each other quietly and once Ellie saw Luke kiss Rachel, then hold her close. Ellie couldn't help watching, trying not to feel jealous. She was too young for Luke, she'd better face it, and anyway there would be plenty of time for all that sort of thing.

Amanda tugged at her sleeve in response to a yell

from the far end of the garden. 'Come on! Bill's starting on the fireworks!'

And they watched together as the first rocket took off with a great zipping swoosh, arching overhead to spill scarlet flowers into the sky.

More Orchard Black Apples

☐ Break Time	*Linda Newbery*	1 84121 584 8	£4.99
☐ Windfall	*Linda Newbery*	1 84121 586 4	£4.99
☐ If Only I'd Known	*Jenny Davis*	1 84121 789 1	£4.99
☐ Falling for Joshua	*Brian Keaney*	1 84121 858 8	£4.99
☐ Balloon House	*Brian Keaney*	1 84121 437 X	£4.99
☐ Bitter Fruit	*Brian Keaney*	1 84121 005 6	£4.99
☐ Family Secrets	*Brian Keaney*	1 84121 530 9	£4.99
☐ Get A Life	*Jean Ure*	1 84121 831 6	£4.99
☐ Just Sixteen	*Jean Ure*	1 84121 453 1	£4.99
☐ Wolf Summer	*Andrew Matthews*	1 84121 758 1	£4.99

Orchard Black Apples are available from all good bookshops,
or can be ordered direct from the publisher:
Orchard Books, PO BOX 29, Douglas IM99 1BQ
Credit card orders please telephone 01624 836000
or fax 01624 837033
or e-mail: bookshop@enterprise.net for details.

To order please quote title, author and ISBN
and your full name and address.
Cheques and postal orders should be made payable to 'Bookpost plc.'
Postage and packing is FREE within the UK
(overseas customers should add £1.00 per book).

Prices and availability are subject to change.